THE

Copyright © 2024 Mage's Moon Publishing.

### THE COMPANY

Written by Joseph S. Samaniego.

Published by Joseph S. Samaniego, 2024

Mage's Moon Publishing

This is a work of fiction. Names, characters, businesses, places, events and incidents are the products of the author's imagination or used fictitiously. Any resemblance to actual persons, living or dead, or actual events is purely coincidental.

No part of this book may be reproduced or transmitted in any form or by any means, electronic or mechanical, including photocopying, recording, or by any information storage and retrieval system, without permission in writing from the publisher.

Maps and Cover created by

Joseph S. Samaniego

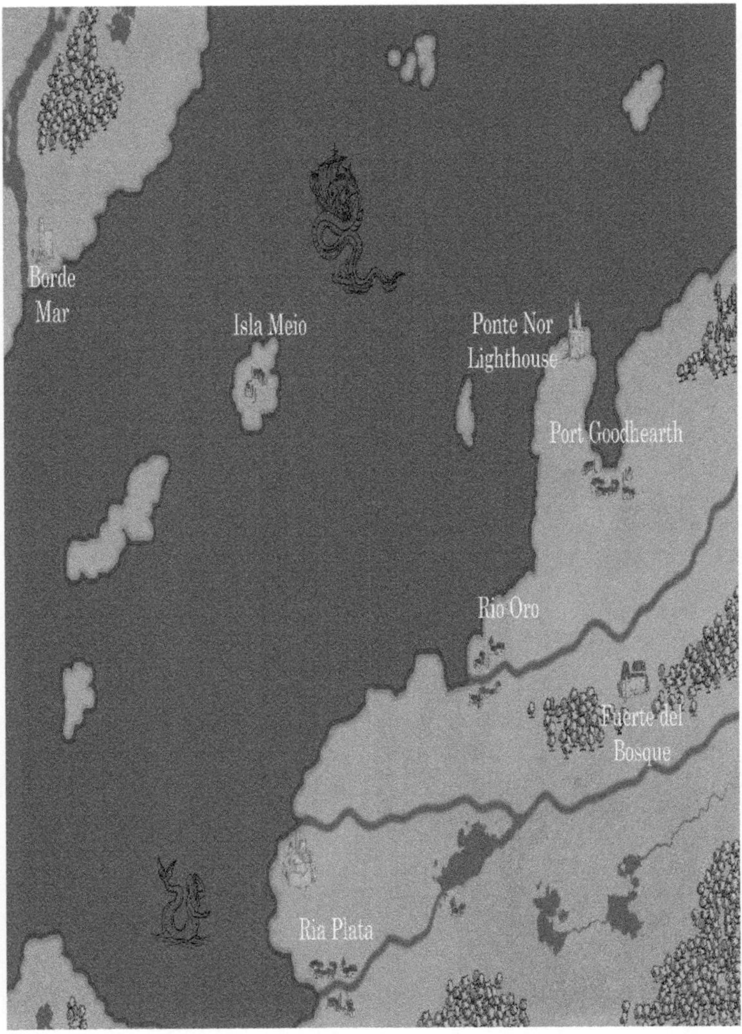
Borde
Mar
Isla Meio
Ponte Nor
Lighthouse
Port Goodhearth
Rio Oro
Fuerte del
Bosque
Ria Plata

Zaragoza

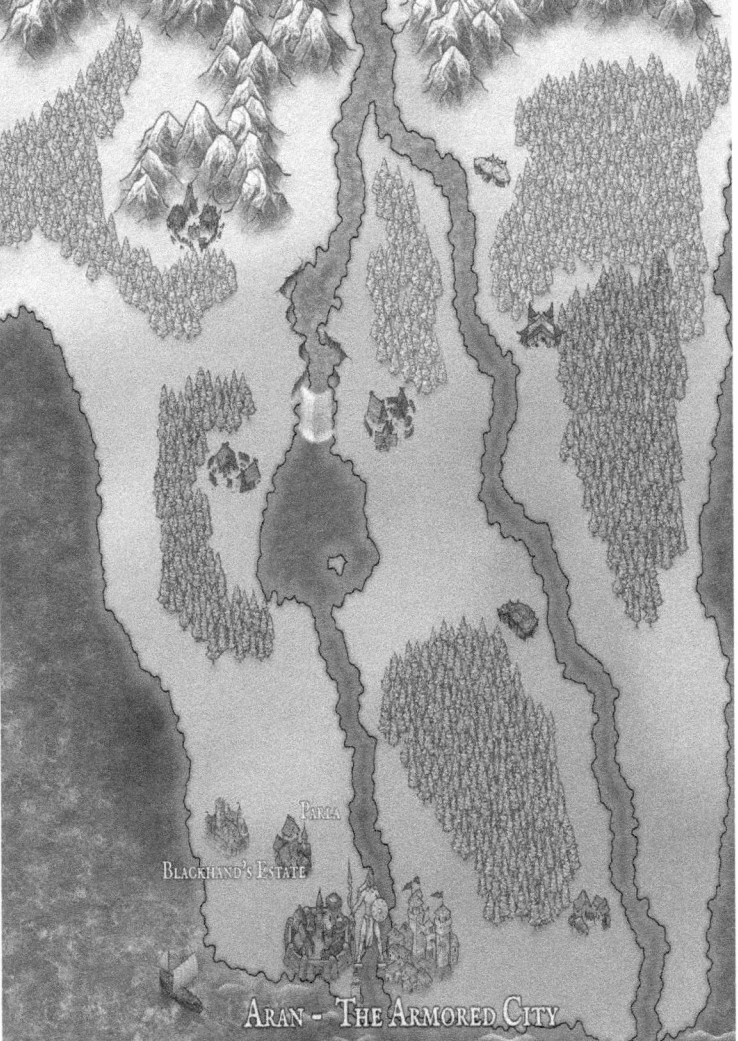

## Table of Contents

| | |
|---|---|
| 1. | 1 |
| 2. | 20 |
| 3. | 31 |
| 4. | 47 |
| 5. | 63 |
| 6. | 80 |
| 7. | 91 |
| 8. | 104 |
| 9. | 123 |
| 10. | 139 |
| 11. | 153 |
| 12. | 170 |
| 13. | 180 |
| 14. | 187 |
| About the Author | 195 |

# I.

*Honor is everything. Without it, the entire system crumbles into dust.*

*Three decades ago, twenty disgraced knights from some forgotten backwater shithole kingdom set off to make something of themselves. It was a risk; it wasn't the best idea, but all they knew how to do was fight and win. Within those thirty years, the twenty knights had built a mercenary company that numbered nearly forty thousand strong and had operations in twenty-three nations. Those knights, minus a few brave knights that fell in past wars, had formed an elite fighting unit, and soon it was booming into a full-fledged mercenary, banking, and commerce empire. It once had a name that has been all but forgotten. After so many years, it had become known simply as The Company.*

\* \* \* \* \*

"I hate working with him. He is a right awful cunt," Blackhand said to his second in command, Sergio de la Espada, known as the Iron Prefect. "He has Longknife as a captain, not one of mine."

Sergio was a thin, but muscular man with a short beard, trimmed to less than an inch, and shortcut hair. He looked more ethnically tied to the southern nations with a slightly more bronze complexion and darker hair than Blackhand.

"And yet, Lord Conrad says we have no choice but to send troops and gold to *Jefe* Antonio," Sergio replied, handing the order documents to Blackhand.

Blackhand inspected the order and scoffed.

"Conrad wants me leading the force."

"Lord Conrad," Sergio corrected.

"Yes, yes. *Lord* Conrad," Blackhand smirked. "I voted for Duke Felipe."

"I remember, sir."

"No matter, Lord Conrad is the *Patrón*, so we have to do as he orders," Blackhand said, leaving the papers on his desk. He looked at Sergio, his castellan, who was effectively the second in command. "Send for a messenger. I have something that will need to go directly to Lord Conrad, and to do that, I must arrange a meeting through his castellan."

Sergio bowed and then exited the room to follow his boss' orders.

Blackhand sat back in his chair and rested his forehead in his hand. It was a unique situation that he found himself in. He was a *jefe* within The Company, and he was comfortable in his seat of power around a geographic region, under Duke Filipe Millan. This was a position that afforded Blackhand, authority, money, and respect. Under him, several captains would run operations in the cities and towns they controlled. Usually in the forms of smuggling, gambling, protection, and mercenaries. Some dealt with mind-altering substances, and others in the oldest profession of providing temporary comfort. Blackhand in turn controlled each of the captains, taking a portion of the profits, and he had earned every bit by being a successful provider and a victor himself. Whether through commerce or in battles, few could claim as many victories as he.

Blackhand sighed. He rubbed his dark brown beard, speckled with strands of red. He had let it grow around four inches in length. While he kept his hair short along the sides and back, he preferred to let the top grow a little longer, giving him something to run his hands through when he felt anxious.

"That damned Antonio can't run a mercenary band to save his life, and now I have to step in for him," Blackhand scoffed. "What will his captains think? It's bad for business when others *have* to step in."

He looked around his office. The only other thing making any noise was the crackling logs in the fireplace.

Blackhand threw his hands up in frustration. "And now I'm talking to myself because of it. I need a vacation."

Two hours later, Blackhand was on his way to his estate, riding in a carriage with Sergio. The dirt road provided a slightly bumpy ride, and the air was crisp. The winter season was setting in, and the temperatures had already started to drop. The cooler air was even more noticeable at night.

"We'll leave at first light in the morning. Pack for a southern summer," Blackhand said.

"Vasha. A despicable place," Sergio mentioned.

Blackhand glanced out the window of the carriage. "It is," he said, not looking at his associate. "But it is one we have to bring back into the fold. *Jefe* Antonio is fucking it up."

Sergio was less than enthused. "It's ruled by damn oligarchs. Vasha oligarchs." Sergio sneered at the words.

"Yeah, they are the worst."

"Especially Count Yuri," Sergio added. "He rules the lot of them with an iron fist."

"And he is why *Jefe* Antonio can't move in completely. Which is why we're heading to the hellhole Vasha in the middle of the summer," Blackhand grinned. "Those temperatures can make Hell seem cold. Aran was good to us, but it will soon be time to pull up stakes, so off we sail to the next job."

Sergio pulled a wrapped bundle from his satchel. "Before I forget, this is the latest take from here in Aran."

Blackhand accepted the wrapped bundle, knowing its lucrative contents. "Thank you," he replied before putting it in his own canvas bag.

The carriage continued on down the road, bumping up and down from the uneven path. It was a main trade road that ran through the city of Parla, and directly to the old fortress that Blackhand used for his home. He often found old castles, fortified and historic, to use for homes until he was sent somewhere else.

Arriving at the main gate, Blackhand and his entourage found a messenger waiting for them.

"*Jefe* Gerald Blackhand?" the man, atop a brown horse, asked.

The rider was dressed in all black, with the Company's sigil on his left breast and Duke Millan's sigil on the right side. He had a small crew of men around him. All dressed the same.

"I have a message from Duke Felipe Millan."

Blackhand exited his carriage, Sergio close behind, a dagger in his right hand by his side. Sergio stepped up and retrieved the message for Blackhand and then sheathed the blade.

Messengers in the night were not very common, and never to be ignored, nor taken lightly.

Blackhand opened the letter and read it to himself. He looked up at Sergio.

"Sergio, send Captain Cortes down to Vasha. We won't be able to make it."

Sergio gave Blackhand an odd look. "Lord Conrad gave an order."

"And Duke Millan has superseded that order. "We have to prepare for our duke's arrival," Blackhand answered, holding up the missive.

Ten days later, with Blackhand and his entourage looking on, Duke Millan stepped off his caravel ship dressed in his finest fur and leather coat, emblazed with his personal coat of arms on the left breast. His attire, right down to his trousers, was of the finest materials, in this case imported high thread Biset cotton pants and a fine silk tunic. His gold rings shone in the bright sun and the golden livery collar marked the focal point of his outfit. It was that collar which told the world he was important and that he had status. Those that knew the heraldry of the double golden wine goblets and skull on a black field knew it to mean that he was a high-ranking member of the Company. As a duke, he was one of nineteen men under the *Patrón* of the Company.

He stood on the dock for a moment surveying the port and the ships lining the dockyard, his salt and pepper hair wafting slightly in the sea breeze, before walking toward where Blackhand was standing. Millan was right around six feet tall, not too stocky, but his weight had increased since his time away from the battlefields.

He was a duke now, and that alone gave him the freedom to send other men and women to fight battles while he stood behind and watched. However, his scars, given to him over decades of fighting in wars, were very much present and a reminder that he was not one to challenge. At least not easily.

He greeted Gerald Blackhand with a nod and an extended hand. Gerald took the hand and kissed the Company ring in one fluid bow.

"Welcome to the Armored City, capital of Aran and the seat of the Sile Empire," Gerald said, lifting from his bow.

"Thank you for your hospitality," Millan said as the pair walked toward the dockside market. "I trust it isn't too much of a burden."

Gerald grinned and gave a soft chuckle. "Not at all, my lord. We are happy to host you for as long as you wish."

Millan stopped, turned to Gerald, and smiled. He placed his left hand on Gerald's right shoulder. "I'm happy to hear it, but I always want to be sure. I was once in your position, and I know what you have to go through when your duke visits."

"Thank you, sir. However, I am always happy when you come. We have a great time," Gerald laughed.

Millan laughed along with Gerald as the pair continued their walk. Up ahead, Sergio held the carriage door open for the two men.

"My lords," he bowed as the men entered the carriage. He followed them in and sat next to his boss, Blackhand.

In the carriage, Duke Millan held a stoic expression. The vehicle moved along the stone road and through the city, bumping and jostling along the route.

"I understand you were ready to move to Vasha, but that's not the best plan right now," Millan said, breaking the usual protocol of pleasantries and starting with business right away. "Lord Conrad isn't seeing that right now. His mind, it is, how do your people say, he has ghosts in his brain."

Gerald Blackhand, a man not of Paisluna heritage, understood the meaning of 'your people'. Often, the dukes would remind their subordinates that they weren't the same. Even Sergio wasn't fully of the same heritage but was half with his father being from the Paisluna region.

"I mean to say he is not fully well. Mentally," Millan added. "He is plotting too dangerously with our men that aren't blooded."

Gerald nodded. "I see. So, having us move?"

"It was a ploy to kill you."

Gerald and Sergio both were shocked.

"He is trying to get rid of everyone that's not Paisluna blood. A few dukes agree with him, but I, and a few more dukes, we'd rather keep our current organization as it is. We are making more money this way," Millan reassured the two men. "More money, and more victories mean more influence for the organization. I have the backing of other dukes, and we will stage a coup and place me at the top. Your skills have insured our success."

"I appreciate the confidence," Gerald replied. "Though I do feel that I might have doomed one of my captains to death."

Millan shook his head. "Our friends were able to steer Captain Cortes to safety," he smiled at Gerald. "You are a good earner, and a good leader. Your men respect you and losing men like you would be a bad business deal," Millan added with a smile.

Blackhand and Sergio both eyed the duke, wondering how he knew it was Cortes that was sent. Both decided to remain quiet for the moment.

"So, my lord," Sergio began. "How would we have been killed?"

"The Vasha oligarchs," Millan said, twirling his hand as he spoke. "They made a deal with Lord Conrad to rid the organization of those Conrad felt weren't worthy of their place. That service is in exchange for mercenaries and lower tariffs on some trade goods. The killings have already begun."

"Did this have anything to do with Dukes de Soto and Alarcon's feud?" Blackhand asked.

"That feud didn't help," Millan replied. "It left an unpleasant taste in many mouths. Mostly because those doing the bulk of the killing were not blooded. It was seen as an insult to have the Paisluna blood members, full members, killed by those with less blood or none at all."

"Mouries, and his family," Blackhand reasoned.

"Them, and a few others," Millan answered. "It shouldn't have been so shocking since they were all assassins to begin with."

Sergio nodded. "But to use them on full Company nobles is a different action than using them as enforcers against nonmembers."

"Correct," Millan said. "An insult to the noble heritage," he added while peering out of the carriage window.

Blackhand narrowed his eyes, looking at Millan. "My lord," he said, drawing his boss' attention. "Were you insulted in any way?"

Millan chuckled and shook his head. "Not at all. We stayed out of the conflict, and I have always lived by the philosophy that's it is better to make an income instead of making enemies."

Blackhand nodded. "I agree," he sighed. "I'm assuming that we have another card to play in this matter."

"We do. In fact, that card is in play right now. I've sent two captains with ten thousand soldiers to Vasha. You won't be leading it, but two blooded captains are. They will subdue any violence from the oligarchs and then turn the country to our control," Millan said. "You and Sergio will stay here for now, but in a fortnight, I need you both to venture to Sala in the realm of Zaragoza. They've been neglecting their tributes, and we need to bring them back to heel. Once that is done, and in the spring, I will have you gather your entire family of soldiers and move them to the south. There, you will await further instructions."

"How far south?" Blackhand asked.

"Ria Plata."

"That's the home country," Sergio said, a bit confused.

Blackhand shook his head. "That could be seen as an act of aggression."

Duke Millan grinned. "And it will be. But prior to your arriving, I have a meeting with the other dukes. It's time to come together to square up any irregularities and misunderstandings. We're also installing four new dukes. Once that's done, I think we'll have a new world in front of us."

## 2.

"I don't like it," Sergio said as he and Blackhand sat at a small table in a tucked away room in Blackhand's castle home. "Duke Millan knows more than we've reported, and his plan puts us in the open."

"I agree," Blackhand nodded. "Sala, nor any other city in Zaragoza, has ever provided tribute. We have no connections there, so that's a lie to begin with."

Sergio gritted his teeth. "This whole thing isn't right. I don't like it."

"Nor I, however, we have an order from our superior. How do we get out of it?" Blackhand asked.

Sergio stood up and walked to the buffet style table and poured two goblets of red wine. "It feels like he is going to set us up just like Lord Conrad wanted to, but only after we do his dirty work for him," he handed a goblet to Blackhand. "It's what I would do."

Blackhand took the goblet and nodded. "That would be my plan, as well. It seems Millan slipped up by saying he brought Cortes back. How did he know to reach out to him before I brought it up?"

Sergio nodded. That key detail was a bit of an eye-opening tidbit. "Then we agree that Duke Millan, for all his grandstanding about our various crews making money and that we are worth living, is lying to us and only wants to use us?"

Blackhand looked at Sergio. He knew his right-hand man was as honorable as they came. Both had fought in battles together and been through hells that others could only have nightmares about. Yet, at that moment, he felt clouded. Blackhand stood from his seat and turned to the window. Foggy glass panes obscured his vision. He turned back toward Sergio.

"Ready our crews. We'll follow Duke Millan's orders in step. In the meantime, I'll send word to any I feel might be loyal to living, particularly those without blood, and see what sort of preemptive moves we can make."

Sergio bowed and then walked out of the room, leaving Blackhand to ponder more than he wanted to. He thought of where exactly Sergio would stand. Sergio was half-blooded, which in the eyes of the dukes, and those full members, wasn't good enough, but maybe in a purge of those without a drop of Paisluna blood, it might do. Self-preservation could be the motivation that Sergio needed to turn on Blackhand, or maybe their blood, shed throughout the years together, might be the leverage that Blackhand could use.

The next morning, Blackhand found Sergio busy with the preparations for a large expedition to Zaragoza. Sala, a small realm within the larger conglomerate of city-states, was a well-fortified capital, and a known area of violence. Millan, after a little prodding by Blackhand, claimed to have brokered some half-assed deal for tribute some years back. A deal that was probably never meant to be made good on if it even existed, and now he was sending Blackhand to hold up their end. That was odd, sending a *jefe* instead of an enforcement crew.

"Between you and me," Blackhand said to Sergio later on as the pair was overseeing the ship, pulling his trusted friend to the side. "We're taking a different route to Zaragoza. We will sail east, down the Central Continent and make a supply stop off in Monrova. We might need a mage."

"And you burned the bridge to our usual mage contact. One that would be on the way to Zaragoza."

Blackhand nodded. "Yes, Fatima is no longer available to me," he sighed. "I wasted an opportunity to further advance our gains, along with personal gains. However, in Monrova there is a *jefe*, a mage in fact, that could also be of help. He isn't blooded either. But he is fiercely loyal to Duke Marques."

"So, we want to pull him into a plot against the dukes?" Sergio asked. "Not sure how, given his loyalty."

"I'm not sure yet, but I want to gauge his opinion on all of this," Blackhand replied.

Sergio nodded his head and returned to his work.

Within days, the pair were out to sea with Blackhand's personal guard of forty huscarls, made from warriors from Aran, Lotcala, and Amazon, among other countries. All armored head to toe for war. Blackhand stood on the prow of his large galley, sailing southwest toward the western shore of the Central Continent.

Sergio stood atop the stern castle, watching the shoreline flow by as they sailed past small port villages and a mountainous shoreline. It wasn't always a dangerous life. Though the seas held their own threats, Sergio loved the water and the salt air. Blackhand walked toward him, passing oarsmen and under the large yardarm of his ship.

"You seem vexed, my friend," Blackhand said as he stopped beside his second in command.

Sergio gritted his teeth. "Noticeable?"

"Only when I look at you."

The pair chuckled at the remark. Sergio heaved a breath and gripped the railing.

"It's just that if we go through with this plan, whether the dukes want to be rid of anyone who isn't blood or not, then we are starting a war. A war that we have to win, or we will die," Sergio spoke up.

"Every war is one we have to win."

Sergio shook his head. "Gerald, you're confusing the fact that we've won every war we've fought in, with a war that we must win. We have also always had the luxury of picking a side."

Blackhand nodded but remained silent.

"I'm with you, *compa*, all the way, but you should know that I am worried," Sergio said. "These are the dukes and their armies. Even if some join us, we're still taking about thousands of warriors following their *jefes* and other blood captains or soldiers."

"I know, Sergio. And while I'm not sure just how many soldiers we'll be up against, I know for a fact that we are going to start a war with the dukes. However, I think it's time for a new head of this family that we call The Company. A new *Patrón*."

"You?"

Blackhand smirked. "If voted on by the remaining *jefes* and *soldados*. Maybe we do things differently. More voices coming together to decide on Company matters. Maybe we have a council instead of one man."

Sergio nodded softly, understanding the idea. "So, we're keeping the voting structure. No moves unless sanctioned and voted on by the dukes, or whatever they'll be?"

"Yes, but I think we keep the titles, just install new people in those roles. However, before we leave here, we need to cull the herd. Make sure that everyone and all the crews, captains, everyone are loyal. Once it's all said and done, we will have to deal with reprisals, so we'll have to take out any that aren't willing to accept the new management."

Sergio's eyes widened. The realization hit him instantly. "Consider it done," he said, with a nod to Blackhand.

The galley ship sailed through mostly calm waters until it finally sailed close to the destination. There, in a protected cape, was the port city of Larsale. One of the biggest profitable cities within The Company's control, and an important port of call for traders, militaries, and pirates. Money, from one source or another, legal or illegal, flowed into Larsale by the millions. It was a city that had to stay in The Company's control.

Blackhand and Sergio stepped onto the docks, along with their forty huscarls. They made their way up the cobblestone streets toward a large tavern owned by *Jefe* Jack 'of All Trades' Kelly. Most just called him Jack or *Jefe* Jack.

Jack was infamous for his magical skills in solving labor disputes and trade negotiations, often with very strong-arm tactics. It was no secret that Jack was the enforcer for Duke Marques' crew. Meaning that he might not be easy to convince, but without him, Blackhand would have to fight an uphill battle.

## 3.

The tavern wasn't as rowdy as one might expect. The patrons of the establishment were mostly dock workers and working men, along with more than a few women plying their wares of the flesh. Blackhand and Sergio walked in, leaving the huscarls outside as security. The pair walked past more than a few known soldiers. Blackhand tilted his head in a nod to the men, all of whom eyed him and Sergio. Around them, patrons and others were enjoying lively games of chances, putting sizeable sums of gold and silver coins down, hoping to get lucky at dice, cards, or fighting of some sort. Usually, dogs were put into a ring fighting bears to the death.

In the back, they came up to a wooden door that Blackhand knew was

Jack's office. He knocked twice. After a moment, the door opened and there stood a beautiful, dark-haired woman. Amazon based on her muscle mass.

"Fucking Blackhand!" a voice behind the woman said. "Let them in."

The Amazon woman stood aside as Blackhand and Sergio entered the large office. Behind an oak desk sat Jack of All Trades Kelly. He was not pleasant to look at with an almost evil glare and a few scars on his clean-shaven face. His reputation helped to fuel his conquests. Over the years, Jack had been successful in various operations, ranging from weapons smuggling, hiring out mercenaries, and fencing stolen goods. He was so successful that he was known to have fenced a king and offered a loan on the collateral of the king's own royal jewels. Those jewels were actually forgeries that

Jack himself had put in place because he had already stolen the authentic royal jewels.

Rumor or not, Jack was not to be taken lightly, but in recent years, Blackhand was thinking that Jack was letting his ego get to him, though Blackhand would not tell Jack that.

Jack eyed the pair of visitors. "You two are not in your territory. This is Marques' turf, and you know the rules about crossing lines. I never got any request asking for permission, so I must ask you, to what do I owe the pleasure of this unannounced and untimely visit?"

Blackhand bowed and then stood back up. "I understand that me and Sergio being here unannounced is a breach of the code. I would have sent a letter to announce this visit, but I couldn't risk it."

Jack smirked.

"I see you have a new guard here," Blackhand said, motioning to the Amazon woman.

"I do," Jack nodded. "Victor lost his soul to the gods of greed. It wasn't an easy decision, but he had to be removed. Chloe," he motioned to the woman, "she is a friend of ours," Jack smiled.

"How so? The books have been closed for over a year," Sergio said.

Jack smirked. "I had to improvise, but I'm way out here on my own, so once the books reopen, I'll make it official. I trust her with my life, and that's what counts."

Blackhand nodded. "I'll take your word for it," he nodded to the woman before turning back to Jack. "Victor was blood. Did the duke give his blessing?"

Jack's smile faded. He twisted his ruby ring on his index finger. A nervous twitch.

"I didn't think so," Blackhand said.

"What was his response?" Sergio asked.

"He wasn't too thrilled. I softened the blow with some extra silver in his usual shipment," Jack replied.

"You can't take out a blooded without the full blessing of the dukes. All of them," Sergio added.

Jack angrily shot up from his chair. "You think I don't know that?" he roared, "I don't need the *Iron Prefect* to tell me that. Don't you have a peaceful village somewhere to burn?"

Sergio puffed up his chest and looked ready to fight at the insult. Chloe gripped her sword hilt, ready to pull it if her boss so ordered.

"Jack," Blackhand said, putting his hands up to calm the man. "I take it that the reason for my visit may be fortuitous, because I get the feeling that you're beginning to see the writing on the wall."

"Like it was on the wall in the fucking banquet hall of a king!" Jack replied. He ran his hand through his hair. "The duke," Jack shook his head, "yeah, he didn't want to take my request to the others even though I caught Victor stealing from the shipments I send up the ladder. That alone should have been enough of a reason to have him removed. But then I found out that Victor was stealing from my own shipments on Duke Marques' orders. Betrayed by the boss and my righthand."

"Does the duke know you know that part yet?" Blackhand asked.

Jack shook his head.

"What was the last shipment that was sent up the ladder?"

"One thousand pounds of silver, and five hundred pounds of pure poppy powder. On top of the usual gold, silver, and flower. Plus, I gave up territories in the north, which means that I've lost income sources to make all that coinage. In total, I have to send thousands of pounds of material and metal."

"That's a big order that requires a lot of setup and work from the dockhands. Is that the normal?" Blackhand asked.

"It is now that Victor is gone," Jack answered. "It's restitution," Jack paused and sighed, "Truth be told, if these orders keep up my workers or my shops, or both, are going to turn on me in weeks. We can't keep up with the demand. Marques knows as much. It's just a matter of when, not if. I'm already hearing the grumbling," Jack sneered at the thought, while glancing out the window to his left.

Blackhand smiled at Jack. "Then stop sending the shipments and keep what's yours. Distribute it among your crews. Buy back their loyalty by showing them that you have their best interests at heart."

"That's mutiny. I'd be branded a traitor to The Company, and you know that."

"Better than death from your own crew," Blackhand replied.

Jack stared at Blackhand. His eyes pierced through the warmly lit office. Candles and a fireplace kept the light flickering on the wooden walls. Jack's blue eyes shone brightly in the darkness.

"What do you get out of all of this? You're not here simply to help me with advice that I didn't ask for. Hell, you didn't even know about this until you got here today. So, I'll ask you again, as a man that said the same oaths and follows the same code as me, why are you here?" Jack asked.

"My duke has also set me up. Turns out the *patron* wants all non-blooded *jefes* and soldiers gone and removed. Conrad was going to have me killed by Vasha mercenaries of all people. My duke, he had a more honorable way in mind. He wants me to go to Zaragoza, and I'm guessing that one of his assassins would finish me off. We took oaths and follow a code, but those dukes and the others who are blooded are connected in a way we can't be, so in their minds, we are expendable. The Company has gotten big, and the dukes are scared about that growth."

"That's why the books were closed. My father used to talk about times like that when he was alive. They do that to prevent too rapid growth," Sergio added.

Jack sighed. "I felt something was off. Any others that we know of that have been taken out?"

"Not yet, but I'm formulating a plan to keep it from happening. I think that we are able to get ahead of this, but I'll need a few mages, which you are one."

"I'm all ears."

Blackhand pulled the chair in front of Jack's desk and motioned for everyone to sit.

"We gather all the soldiers, *jefes*, all the non-blooded, and any staunch allies, blood or not, to our side and declare war on the dukes," Blackhand said.

Jack's eyes were wide, and his mouth was slightly open.

"An all-out war with the ruling families that have held the crews for years," Sergio added.

"So, if you don't send that shipment, no, the moment that you don't send that shipment, the war will have begun, just like if I don't arrive in Zaragoza within two fortnights. We have that much time before the shit hits."

"We just had a war, and it ended very badly for the non-blooded," Jack said, his head in hand. He felt a heavy burden on his shoulders.

"I know, and now we're about to have another. But this one is for our,"

Blackhand motioned around the room. "Our survival."

Jack nodded. "I can do one fortnight and have my crews prep for the aftermath. Weed off anyone that will talk, of course, but let them know that those are the final two shipments."

"I need two fortnights," Blackhand replied.

Jack looked at Chloe. "Find Morello and bring him to me. I can contract out his crew to outsource the other fortnight."

Chloe nodded and then left to follow the order.

Jack looked and noticed Sergio's concerned face. "She's good. A levy orphan excluded from the Amazonian Herd. I linked up with her a few years ago after she did some fighting around the world, and she's been loyal ever since I brought her in."

"What of this Morello?" Blackhand asked.

"He's the leader of the Old Foxes, a local street gang that usually pays tribute to The Company. We give them extra work at times. They don't have loyalty to the dukes and won't know them if they saw any of them. The foxes are just plain and simple criminals. They'll like this," Jack said with a sly grin. "They like collecting and pulling poppy. I'll let them skim a little off the top plus a bonus for getting the job done, and we'll have them in our pocket for when the dukes realize what's happening."

"The name Morello sounds connected."

"Don't worry, Blackhand. It's not, at least not for generations. I knew his father, a good man, but his family has been in Larsale for centuries. Now, let's talk about who else is joining. We need more soldiers."

"I'm heading to Zaragoza, and I was going to stop along the way at Riverport in Tresha. I have a connection with a *jefe* there," Blackhand said.

Jack laughed. "The Rooster."

Blackhand nodded with a grin. "El Gallo. He's another half-blood, like Sergio here," Blackhand motioned to his friend. "He has a strong force there, ships, and a reason to hate the dukes."

"His counterfeiting skills will come in handy, too."

Blackhand grinned. "They will, indeed."

"I'll reach out to another *jefe* I've worked with before. He's out of Duke

Leva's territory in the east. They call him The Butcher, but his mother named him Pete. I'll contact him and bring him on board. He hates the dukes but loves their money. We can count on his loyalty if we pay enough for it. Fair warning though, he's a fucking psycho, hence the name. He is Leva's enforcer and top assassin. He likes to use black powder kegs and doesn't give a shit about collateral damage. But his crew will be the type of soldiers we need," Jack finished and pulled out a bottle of rum and three glasses. He sat the glass on the table and poured the rum in each. "Gentlemen," he said, raising his glass. "To the start of the rest of our lives, however long they might be," he toasted before taking a drink.

Blackhand and Sergio drank theirs and then stood up to leave. Blackhand turned and faced Jack. "Two fortnights, and then we meet in Zaragoza."

Jack nodded before the other two left him alone in his office.

## 4.

Sergio walked to the bow castle of the galley where Blackhand was standing. "Gerald, I've been wondering, why do these *jefes* hate the dukes yet still run the crews for them?"

"They each have their own reasons. We live within a violent world, and as such, we operate in a violent business," Blackhand said with a sigh. "I think a lot of it is choosing the lesser of two evils or just survival through safety in numbers. I can't speak about The Butcher's reasons, however, El Gallo, I know his. His father was killed on the orders from Duke Leva and Torero during the last civil war within the company. He swore a vendetta against them both, but Duke Millan wouldn't let him hold it or act on it. Therefore, Millan made a fatal error."

"Millan always said that everything in the Company was business. Never take anything personal," Sergio replied.

"Tell that to a grieving son," Blackhand added.

Sergio simply nodded at the response. "What about the captains and their blood status? Will they join us just like that?"

Blackhand smiled. "That's the beauty of what we as *jefes* do. We're in the streets and on the battlefields with the captains and soldiers. We bleed with them. That's a whole other kind of loyalty that money won't be able to buy. Once we get to Riverport, we'll send word to Güero and bring him up to speed. He has the most *soldados* at his side and can reach Zaragoza the quickest. Once we have him at our side, the other captains will fill in the gaps as we close around the dukes."

Blackhand smiled at his friend, but Sergio still looked concerned.

"You're still unsure?"

Sergio shook his head. "I'm just trying to lie out all the chess pieces before too many moves are made."

"Well, if you see a good move, be sure to let me know. I've always respected your advice, *amigo*," Blackhand said with a friendly pat on Sergio's shoulder. "That's a mistake that the dukes often make that I don't plan to."

The pair tried to enjoy the rest of the journey. There was not much else for them to do but sit back and wait for the trip to be over. Blackhand had put them behind schedule with his plan, and now the ship was sailing, and rowing, through the wide river that ran through the Central Continent. The Casiendan River and its deep-water tributaries allowed for the shallow hulled galley to traverse through the Treshan Kingdom, or what was left of it after several recent wars. The river still fed the kingdom with lucrative trade and fertile valleys. That was something that Blackhand, his mind always open for new deals, saw as a possible future. However, that would depend on El Gallo. Without his support and agreement, making any deals in Tresha would be seen as encroachment and disrespectful.

Arriving in Riverport at night was not usual, but not too dangerous. Blackhand and Sergio disembarked from their ship, leaving the huscarls behind to guard their ship.

"My standard on that galley will get people talking. We'll head to a high-end tavern and brothel for the night. That'll also bring Gallo to us quickly," Blackhand said.

An hour later, Blackhand and Sergio were enjoying a bottle of whiskey when Gallo, oak cane in hand, and one of his captains burst through the front door. Around them, a few of his soldiers filtered in. The patrons in the tavern all went silent and began to scatter away along with any of the prostitutes that they were flirting with.

"When I was leaving my office this evening, one of my captains, Lobo," Gallo said, pointing to the man on his right, "he told me that Blackhand's flag was flying above a ship that was seen coming into my city. I look at the docks and low and behold, there is Blackhand's personal galley with armed warriors. Those heavily armed warriors then go on to tell me that Blackhand and the Iron Prefect are walking around the city. My city!" Gallo roared, pounding his large barrel-like chest with his fists. "Uninvited and unannounced! Why?"

Blackhand smiled and poured a glass of whiskey. He passed the glass toward the edge of the table and motioned for Gallo to sit down.

"I'm here to see you, Gallo," Blackhand said. He again motioned for the large Gallo to sit. "Apologies, but it had to be in secret."

Gallo slowly sat across from Blackhand and Sergio. Lobo joined them at the table as well. Blackhand poured another glass for him.

"Why are you here, Gerald?"

"Breaking code," Blackhand smirked.

Gallo drank his whiskey. "I see that," he responded in a raspy voice.

"Truth is, I'm gathering intelligence on the status of The Company," Blackhand said.

Lobo smirked. "We heard you were heading to Vasha."

Gallo nodded. "I wondered when you'd be coming," he let out a chuckle, and Lobo turned to his boss, shocked. "Millan ain't backing you up, is he?"

"Millan rearranged the Vasha trip, but he has another dangerous trip in mind. Zaragoza," Blackhand replied.

"Watch out for their blades. I ain't never seen a Zaragozan that did not have a blade on them. Ain't Cortes from the

Zaragoza region? Maybe he should have gone instead."

Blackhand nodded.

"That's the concern," Sergio replied. "More specifically, a Company blade."

Blackhand nodded. "I just came from Jack of All Trades' place. He is working off an impossible debt imposed by his duke. He killed a blooded captain."

"A fucking death sentence. Hate to be him," Gallo said with a hmph. "But that has nothing to do with me or my crew."

"I think you know it does."

Gallo was silent.

Blackhand continued. "It's coming. Some of us always thought it might, especially after the last war. Those blooded men and women want their revenge for what Mouries and his hit squad did. They have a lot of blood on their hands. Pure blood, and the killers, Mouries and his hit squads, weren't of the same 'noble' blood."

"They were all executed."

"Not all," Blackhand replied. "Mouries, and a couple others are still alive. Just hidden. Duke Reyes even went after Mouries' sister attempting to draw out Mouries, but Reyes only ending up getting himself and half his family killed. Six crews all wiped out."

Gallo's eyes widened. "They went after Lestrade *de la Flor Venenosa*? She runs a racket that even The Company doesn't interfere with. She's the best assassin there is."

"Was. Still might be, but now she's married and settling down with a family," Blackhand smiled. "I don't plan on testing her, even if ordered. But back to the business at hand, you have a vendetta against Torero and Leva. I can help with that."

Gallo gritted his teeth. "Millan would never sanction it. He already denied me my rights."

Blackhand shook his head. "Well, what if I told you that I have a reason to not listen to Millan?"

"Your Zaragoza trip?" Gallo asked. "Yea, I wouldn't trust that either. I've heard the rumors."

"A birdy told you?" Blackhand smirked.

"She came in here," Gallo nodded. "Her and that young mage she's teamed up with, they came in a week ago. It wasn't good news, but from what she said, the whole south has been purged of any non-blood," he side-eyed Lobo.

Blackhand and Sergio took the cue.

"What else did she say?" Blackhand asked, bring the conversation back.

"To watch my back. She said that the blooded members had orders to take us non-bloods out. We talked in private and said the snakes have crept too close," he again side eyed his captain sitting next to him.

Lobo scoffed. "She's just spreading rumors. I ain't never trusted them death dealers."

"The dead don't lie, Lobo," Blackhand smirked. "Blooded men do."

Without a second of hesitation, Sergio flung a small knife at Lobo, piercing the man in the heart, letting the traitorous captain fall dead onto the table. The *soldados* behind Gallo rushed forward, but Gallo stood up and cast a spell, freezing the *soldados* in place.

"Stop!" Gallo yelled. "Lobo wasn't a friend of ours. He stopped being one when he took Vashan gold."

Gallo reached into the dead Lobo's pocket and pulled out a gold coin and threw it down on the table. The coin was stamped with the Vashan crest. He released the spell, let his *soldados* down. The men calmed down and sat back in their places behind their boss.

"How deep does all this run?" Sergio asked, picking up the coin.

"Based on Fatima's intel, and from what I've learned from various sources, Conrad owes a lot of money to the Vasha oligarchs, and he can't clear the debt without taking our businesses for himself," Gallo said. "Fatima told me to contact you, but then we heard you were sent out to Vasha. I'm glad that wasn't the case."

"No, but it's not much better. The dukes are in on this. But Conrad will kill them next. It never ends with just one," Blackhand said. "Look, we need to clear our loyalties now. Jack is with us and he's bringing the Butcher in, as well."

"Pete the Butcher?" Gallo's eyes widened. "That's Duke Leva's top enforcer."

"Jack says that he's willing to turn for money."

Gallo shook his head. "It'll take more than money for him to turn. Pete bleeds loyalty."

"Then why did Jack say he'd turn?" Sergio asked.

Gallo shrugged. "Unless Jack has something on Pete that is worth more than gold, I couldn't even tell you what would make him think that. Pete killed his own brother on Duke Leva's orders. Strangled him from behind when he was released in a prisoner exchanged. Leva claimed it was because the brother talked about Company business while Pete was locked up, but most of us know it was a loyalty test. Pete passed."

"That is not good for us," Blackhand said, with a dour look. "Jack is either walking into a trap or he's walking us into one."

"We might need to recruit another *jefe* or two and their crews then," Sergio said, thinking of a contingency plan considering the new information.

"I know of one," Gallo said. "She'll need help, so we'd have a favor on her."

"La Elfa?" Blackhand asked, already thinking of their mutual contacts.

Gallo nodded. "She's locked up in Corona Prison right now and Duke Torero is letting her languish, even though she's running her crews from the prison without missing a step. If it ain't broke, he won't fix it, but it ain't right to leave her in there."

"Well, let's break her out and get a favor. From what the stories say, she's a powerful mage," Blackhand said.

"She is, when there isn't a silver locket with an iron and salt vial embedded in her back," Gallo replied. "We get her out, and that locket out of her, then we can get La Elfa and all of her crews and *soldados*. We just need someone that can rip that thing out without killing her."

"Not just someone," Sergio said. "A powerful mage."

"I think I know someone," Blackhand smiled.

# 5.

Verix sat alone in a small room just south of Reposo. He had broken amicably from Geddoe's dragon hunting group a month prior, and now he wanted a break. He needed more time to heal from his mental anguish. Cailin and Fatima had made good on the promises that Lestrade and Amasis had made to Geddoe to help revive him, but Verix had already awoken. He was happy his friend had looked out for him, and he readily rejoined him for a short time, but Verix was still worn out and tired. His once naturally tanned skin was now paler and sicklier. Verix's dreams had turned to darkness again, and he knew why.

His magical arts were going to be needed again, and to do something burdensome.

That's about the time that Blackhand had reached out to him, and so now he sat in a small room in Reposo waiting for Blackhand to show up.

The waiting wasn't the worst part. The headaches were. Headaches that now required poppy powder. That was a detriment, but one that Verix had to have. So much of it made him cling to it and yearn for it. He couldn't function without a daily dose of poppy powder, and that dose was increasing each day. Still, he needed every bit of it. At least, that's what he told himself with each and every dose.

"The visions must be calmed," Verix would say in a trembling voice as he poured more powder into his wine.

It had been over two years since his awakening, and in that time, he had gained little of his former life back. He looked disheveled and weak. He had lost a lot of weight, and his once thick, dark brown hair had thinned out considerably and lightened to almost fully grey. That was unusual for someone still in their early thirties. His beard was scraggly and unshaven, with a distinct lack of care.

His best friend Geddoe would check in on him from time to time, however, no one, except for Geddoe, would believe the fanciful stories that he kept repeating. All the visions he kept seeing from the time that his mind was merged with the elder dragon's. Even after the dragon was killed for its dark purpose, the magic residue that was left behind festered in Verix's mind.

Verix sat in a dark corner of the tavern, counting his few coins, wondering how he would pay for his next meal. He had been able to beg for some coins and with a few simple magic tricks, Verix conned some more money from people, but he wasn't sure how long that would last. How fortuitous it was that a familiar, though long-lost, face entered the tavern.

Verix's eyes widened as Blackhand and Sergio came to his table and sat down with him.

"You're a hard man to find. Took me a few more hours than I could really spare. I sure hope you can help me make that time up when we travel to Zaragoza," Blackhand said.

"I…I've been he…here for some time, Blackhand," Verix shakingly replied.

"Yes, I finally figured that out. Geddoe wouldn't tell me, but a few of his crew are more easily persuaded with shiny coins."

Sergio shook his head. "What's the point of having a crew if someone else can buy them?"

Blackhand smirked. "Indeed," he pulled out a glass vial from his coat and sat it on the table in front of Verix. "I need your help, Verix. I can pay you in gold and silver, or in this."

"What's that?" Verix asked.

"The headaches are getting worse, I imagine. You've been on this stuff for so long now that it's taking multiple doses a day. What are you up to now?"

Verix sat quietly.

"I'm guessing, just by looking at you and seeing you shaking there, again it's just a guess, but I'd say four doses," Blackhand said. "That must be hard, with the Knights of the Silver Seal coming down hard on mages, and the trade of mind dulling and altering substances. Turns out they also want to stop the trade of poppy powder, meaning that it's got to be increasingly difficult for you to get your regular doses."

Verix remained quiet.

"I don't have time for this silent treatment, so here are all my cards. I have to break someone, a powerful mage, out of Corona Prison. She's locked and can't perform magic, so I need a strong mage that can break that lock. Then I have to be in Zaragoza to be assassinated," Blackhand paused as Verix seemed to be shocked at the last statement. "Don't concern yourself with that part. I'll be fine, but that's why I'm being sent there. The Company wants me dead, and I want to, correction, I need to prevent that. However, I need to be in Zaragoza in three days and it would be at least a month to sail there from here. Therefore, you'll need to portal us there. My ship and all."

Verix sat, staring blankly with his mouth wide open.

"Take a moment, please," Blackhand said, rolling his eyes.

"Verix, we have to move quickly. We can help you with the poppy. Whether you want to be rid of it, or you want more of it. Either way, we can help you and in exchange for that help, you will help us break our contact out of prison," Sergio explained.

Verix reached for the vial and popped the cork. He looked in and then put the cork back. Verix nodded.

"I'm not sure what I want, but I'll help and let you know one way or another soon," Verix said, pocketing the vial.

Blackhand stood, followed by Sergio and Verix. "Good. Now let's head to Corona and break La Elfa out so we can take on the Company."

"Hurry, the knights are increasing their patrols, and I haven't seen them yet this morning, so they'll be coming soon," Verix said, rushing the others along with him.

Verix and the pair of Company men stepped out of the tavern and ducked down a side alley. There, Verix conjured a portal that would put them near the infamous prison. The three stepped through the portal just as a patrol of silver seal knights walked by.

*****

"We're just a mile away, but they have wards, so this is as close as we're going to get," Verix said, adjusting his purple cloak. He had been able to portal Blackhand, Sergio, and himself close to Corona prison.

"Then how are we going to get inside the walls?" Sergio asked.

"Someone is going to have to be a decoy, and we'll need a wagon," Blackhand said.

Two hours later, Sergio and Verix were driving a horse-drawn carriage to the main gate of the prison. Blackhand was sitting in the back. Each had a Knight of the Silver Seal crest on their cloaks. The wagon pulled up to the gate and was then stopped by the prison guards.

"Halt! State your business here!"

Sergio looked over at the guard and handed him a writ with the knightly order's wax seal.

"We're here to retrieve an elf mage from the prison. Wanted for murder and the king has given her over to us," Sergio said.

The guard looked at the writ. Fresh black ink, with the king's own signature, and a hardened wax stamped seal. Hard to forge, but unusual. The guard looked at his fellow guards and showed them the parchment. After a few minutes of talking amongst themselves, the guard waved them in.

Sergio whipped at the two horses and the wagon moved further into the prison, where the three hopped off and walked toward another set of guards.

"Whatever magic you can do, cloud their ability to use any obsidian mirrors,"

Blackhand whispered over his shoulder to Verix.

Verix nodded and then whispered a quick spell.

That would buy them a short amount of time.

"Let's hope they don't catch on," Verix added.

"The knights have crests that block magic, and we'll use that excuse until we can't anymore," Sergio replied.

The trio were led around the prison, past different quads and housing blocks where inmates were kept. More than a few were mages that were blocked from using their powers. Blackhand lowered his head under the knightly cowl, trying to hide his face, as he walked past the cells and open areas. In some of the open areas, inmates were exercising and socializing with others. Their loyalties were obvious, with a strict hierarchy of gangs associating among different crews.

One guard walked with them. He didn't seem as rough around the edges as the other guards from the front gate.

"To get to this prisoner, the elf lady, we have to go to the high security quad," the guard said as they walked.

The group walked to a large stone building that looked like a castle. There, they waited for the guard to confer with the other guards and opened the front door. It was a massive oak door with wards against magic. The group walked in under the watchful gaze of the remaining guards. Walking into the ward was an act of courage in itself. The halls were dark, damp, and cold. There weren't any exterior windows in the halls, nor in the cells, giving the whole interior a dark atmosphere that was only and dim, lit by small torches. The walls were solid stone, with only one small window for each cell, and a short door that anyone would have to crouch down to walk through.

"I'm guessing that the prisoner doesn't get many visitors," Blackhand joked.

The guard nodded. "These are the most dangerous inmates and only get one hour a day outside. No visitors. This one is particularly dangerous. I can understand why the knights want her."

The group found La Elfa's cell at the end of the hallway. The guard knocked on the door of the cell.

"Hey there, these knights are coming to transfer you to their own prison."

They heard a shuffling within the cell, and the guard peered in the window to see the prisoner standing there.

"Get your bedroll and clothes. Pack it up!"

Blackhand looked around the hall and saw that it was empty.

"Allow us," he said before knocking the guard out.

The guard fell to the ground with a hard clump, his helmet echoing down the hall.

"How much do you want to bet that the other guards might have heard that?" Sergio asked.

"Verix, mind control him and get him up."

Verix warded the fallen man, standing him up and then entered his mind.

"This might make it hard if we have to get him to talk."

"Then let's hurry," Blackhand said, pulling the keys from the guard's belt. He unlocked the door, and crouched down, but didn't enter. "La Elfa," he softly called into the cell. "I'm with The Company. Name's Gerald Blackhand. Sergio and I here are going to get you out."

The elf woman stuck her head through the door. Her blonde hair wrapped around her face, a large scar ran down the left side of her face and over where her left eye once was. In place of her eye was a black orb.

"Blackhand?" La Elfa chuckled. "Who sent you?"

"El Gallo. We need your help with an operation," Blackhand answered.

La Elfa crawled through the doorway, with Sergio closing it behind her. "If it gets me out of here, sure, but there's something I'll need as well."

"The locket?" Sergio asked.

La Elfa shook her head. "No, I need help getting rid of interlopers on my turf. Help me with that, and I'm in."

"Okay, now we walk out. Put the chains on her," Blackhand said, "We have to make it look legit," he said, noting the angry look on La Elfa's face.

"Fine, but as soon as we're out of here, they come off."

"Of course," Blackhand said, slipping the chains around her wrists.

The group walked out, with Verix magically leading the stunned guard. They walked past the gate of the high security castle. While nervous, all four plus the stunned guard made it through without incident. After a long and rather unnerving walk past many howling, hollering, and roaring inmates, the group finally made it to the main gate. Blackhand led La Elfa to the wagon while Sergio and Verix walked with the stunned guard off to the side, leaving him propped against the wall.

    Once everyone was in the wagon, the group pushed the horses past the mile radius of the magic barrier. There Verix formed a portal, and the four members walked through and walked out on Blackhand's galley, already en route to Zaragoza.

## 6.

The waves crashed against the galley's side planks as the ship sailed south on the open waters. The sky was clear, and the sea birds were flying high. There was nothing like a bright and sunny day upon the southern waters. Blackhand and Sergio were sitting near the stern with Verix joined the pair, tossing a silver locket lightly in his hand.

"You retrieved the lock, I see," Blackhand said.

Verix nodded. "Not too difficult."

"It wasn't?" Sergio asked.

Verix sat next to the pair. "No, it was rather difficult, actually. False bravado."

"How's La Elfa?" Blackhand asked.

"Tired, and drained. It took its toll, but she'll be okay in a little while. These locks are dangerous. They drain the person of magic, and then it starts draining the life-force. To remove it," Verix sighed. "It hurts the person who it's locked within and the person who's trying to remove it. A fabricated vampire of sorts that takes an overload of magic to remove," Verix sighed. "I'm not sure why I tried to downplay it, or why I'm giving you the full story."

"You're modest," Sergio replied.

"And honest," Blackhand added, handing a bottle of rum to Verix.

"That's probably going to get me killed one day. Especially in this business," Verix smirked, accepting the rum.

Blackhand shook his head. "You'd be surprised, but being honest is the best thing you can be in our world."

Verix shot the pair of Company men a confused and unbelieving look.

"I'm serious. Everyone expects the lie, but no one thinks anyone is being honest. That's why most of us are. If I tell you I'm going to do something, I will do it. If I don't follow through, then my credibility is gone. And without credibility, then I won't be trusted, and without trust, I'm a dead man."

"Doing what you say you are going to do seems more like following through with threats," Verix noted.

"At times it is," Blackhand conceded. "It also means that when I say I'll trust someone or reward their trust, I mean it."

As the three spoke, La Elfa walked through the door of the stern cabin. Verix started moving towards her.

La Elfa held her hand up. "I'm fine."

"You should rest," Verix said.

La Elfa shook her head. "I have to speak with your boss."

"He's not my boss," Verix replied.

La Elfa grinned. "If you say so," she turned to regard Blackhand and Sergio. "You need me to help you, but I need help on my turf."

"I got you out of prison."

"A prison that wasn't keeping me from working for the Company."

Blackhand stood up. "For how long you think that would have continued?"

La Elfa gave him a confused look. "How do you mean?"

Sergio stood up beside his boss. "The dukes are turning on anyone that isn't blooded. That's us, and you. More than a few other *jefes*, too."

"Word from a reputable source is that the south has already been purged. I have a captain in Rio Plata, and I've asked him to look into it," Blackhand added.

"Torero hasn't tried to negotiate to release you? Not once?" Sergio asked, his right eyebrow raised.

La Elfa remained silent.

"I'll take that as a no," Blackhand said. "We, along with a few other *jefes,* are going to stage a coup, but we need *soldados* willing to start fresh."

La Elfa nodded. "Fine, but if I'm going to be worth anything when it's all said and done, I need to have my problem fixed ASAP."

"What's the problem, then?" Blackhand asked.

La Elfa reached for the bottle of rum from Verix. "I run the rackets in Ciudad Topo. Above ground, we've built an empire of protection, powder smuggling, and coinage. We even have the permit to mint copper coins. Under me, I have six captains and over three hundred *soldados*, all non-bloods and mostly elves, and all deadly."

Blackhand grinned and nodded. "Sounds promising."

"It is when the sewer rats don't screw it up."

"Sewer rats?" Sergio asked.

"This one petty thief named *Raton* has moved in on my turf, but he keeps to the sewers and then pops up, quite literally, from the gutters to rob my shipments. He even hijacks my legitimate business shipments. Torero hasn't been happy, and my men haven't been able to find this *Raton* bastard. We get rid of him and then we get the city back, and all the lucrative business. We'll need that minting business if you plan work trade after the coup."

Blackhand looked at Sergio and nodded. "We will. I can't go right now. I have to be in Zaragoza to meet with whatever my duke has in store for me, and to see if Jack of All Trades plans to double-cross me."

"He will. He does it to everyone. Jack's the reason why the last civil war started to begin with," La Elfa replied.

"How so?" Blackhand asked, now feeling perplexed by such new information.

"Jack, under the orders of his duke and Lord Conrad, firebombed a whole non-blooded crew. Then planted a forged note in the office of *Jefe* Hidalgo so he'd get framed for it. Duke Leva, the boss of the crew that was firebombed, ordered Hidalgo killed, and that's when shit got crazy."

"*Jefe* Hidalgo was El Gallo's father!" Sergio responded.

"And Jack is setting us up with Pete the Butcher, who works for Leva," Blackhand said.

"And Pete likes to handle business with black powder kegs," Sergio said.

Blackhand slammed his fist on the ship's side rail. "My money is on Jack leading us into a trap."

"Looks like you're the only honest *jefe* in the Company, Gerald," Verix quipped with a smug grin.

"There's a couple of us," La Elfa answered.

"Those damn Paisluna bastards!" Blackhand yelled out. He sighed and took a second to calm himself. "Fine, we're walking into two traps. One set by Duke Millan and the other set by Jack. El Gallo was already not trusting Jack and Pete, so we can try to find him with an obsidian mirror and warn him to stay back. We'll meet him south of the city. In the meantime, let's find another port of call."

Blackhand left the other three at the stern and found the ship's captain, relaying the orders to dock south of Zaragoza and away from the city.

He rejoined the others on the stern castle shortly after.

"Here's the new plan. Contact Gallo and bring him up to speed, but he wants

Leva's head, and I think we can get it for him. For your rat problem," Blackhand looked directly at La Elfa, "I'll send my best captain," he looked at Sergio. "Second best. Sergio here is the best. Güero will handle it quickly and quietly."

"Fuck that. I want everyone to know I ordered it," La Elfa replied.

"So be it. We'll make sure that it's known, but it'll be handled," Blackhand said. "That also gives us a reason to pull Güero out of Ria Plata where the dukes will be soon."

"That meeting they have each year," La Elfa said. "It's almost winter, I had forgot."

"We can make that work for us, but first we have to gather more *jefes*," Blackhand said.

"I can reach out to a few that I know would join us without hesitation, especially if that means we can keep more off the top," La Elfa replied.

"Do it, and make it quick, before anyone thinks anything is amiss," Blackhand looked to Verix. "You in?"

"Do you need a mage for all of this?" Verix shrugged.

Blackhand, La Elfa, and Sergio all nodded.

Verix said and took the bottle of rum back, turning it up for a large gulp. "Then I'm in," he said with a raspy voice, once finished with the rum.

# 7.

"Blackhand has had a change in plans," El Gallo said to his captains. He was sitting at his wooden desk, with four captains across from him and two others speaking through obsidian mirrors. "I figured that Jack would turn on him."

"How's he want to handle it, then?" one captain asked.

"Yeah, I got really excited when you said he had a plan for us all to be under new management," another captain added.

Gallo nodded and leaned back in his chair. "For now, status quo. We'll move when he gives the word. He's not moving to Zaragoza just yet, and that's when we were going to meet up."

"That's something that he busted La Elfa out for, and now he lost that advantage. It won't be long before Torero finds out about her being free," a third captain laughed.

"Skinny," Gallo said, looking to one of his captains, a rather stout dwarf with dark brown hair and a long beard. "Get me the doc. I need to ask her about something."

"Sure thing, boss," Skinny replied. He, along with the other captains, all left Gallo in his office alone.

Gallo looked at a paper in his hand. It was a missive that he had urgently received from one of Blackhand's captains, a Quarmi man named Shade. He had received the orders just before and used his magical portal to reach El Gallo quickly.

"I hope this works, Blackhand," Gallo said to himself before tossing the missive into the roaring fireplace.

* * * * *

"I think it could work," Sergio said, looking at Blackhand and La Elfa.

"Paper gold?" La Elfa said with a raised eyebrow.

"Not gold, really, but any currency. Paper notes showing the worth of the customer. Easier to carry," Sergio replied, shaking his head.

Blackhand rubbed his bearded chin in thought. "How would it work, exactly?"

Sergio grinned. "Easy. The customer would come to us and give us their gold, silver, copper, bronze, whatever that nation has in rotation. Then we inventory it, give the customer a note or several depending on their preferences, but those slips of parchment would show what they have in our vault. They can then take that to another company crew or family, show the note with the company seal, and withdraw their coinage. With a small fee applied for the convenience."

"Interesting," Blackhand said.

"We can even offer loans against the coinage within the vaults."

"From the customers' coins?" La Elfa asked.

"Yes. That way it frees up Company funds."

"What if they want their money back after we give a loan?" Blackhand wondered.

"Depending on the size of the loan or the size of the withdrawal, it shouldn't be a problem, but we could also stipulate that any withdrawal over a certain amount would take various days to gather," Sergio answered. "That way, we have time to make sure that the gold is always there."

"In some kingdoms, it's illegal to take interest on loans," Blackhand added.

"That's why we'd say it's a holding fee for convenience," Sergio smiled.

Blackhand nodded and grinned. "I like it."

La Elfa smiled. "Then let's win this coming war so we can implement it. I'm all for any plan that will make us money, but we got to live first."

\* \* \* \* \*

"We have days, not weeks, not months, just days to plan this operation," Jack said to a tall man walking beside him in the port city of Zaragoza.

"I have both of the kegs in place. All we need is for everyone to arrive," the man smiled. "Then everything blows big."

Jack stopped to gaze over the docks. He smiled and turned to the man. "Pete, this is the beginning of the best deal we've ever made and once those kegs blow, we'll get everything we've ever deserved."

Pete nodded. "How will we deal with any reprisals from the captains?"

"They join the new regime and the new duke, or they die along with the others," Jack said bluntly. "But first, let's worry about this operation. We have to strike quick to avoid a longer war. This is just the smokescreen that will be the start of the deception."

The pair stood at the docks with their backs to the warehouses and work crews loading cargo. Amongst the workers stood a woman, watching the pair while hauling burlap sacks of trade goods. She blended in with the crowd, her head covered with a brown hood and a worn and ragged cloak. It wasn't strange to see a stone elf woman working on the docks. Usually, one such as a scorned and distrusted stone elf could only find manual labor work.

She hovered around different corners, keeping one eye on the two Company men. As the pair started to leave the area, the elf woman followed, sinking into the shadows and behind crates as they walked. Finally, the pair left the cobblestone street and walked into a tavern. The woman watched as they entered, followed by a few of their soldiers. She turned and went back toward the docks and away from the city.

Several miles south of the city, the elf woman found a secluded smuggler's dock and boarded a weatherworn long galley.

"Both Jack and Pete are there in Zaragoza, boss," she said, walking up to Blackhand. "Just like you said, and they were talking about the kegs around the docks. They're planning a quick strike."

"Thank you, Oreja," Blackhand said to the woman, and handed her a gold coin. Oreja accepted the payment and then rejoined the other huscarls. Blackhand turned back to Sergio and La Elfa. "As La Elfa figured, Jack is going to double-cross us, but what we don't know is if it is for his own gain or for a duke's."

"I can't imagine that he would do it for anyone else but his duke," La Elfa replied.

"Either way, we can't go to the docks. We have to enter Zaragoza by another way," Sergio pointed out.

"I might have a way," Verix said, walking up. "It'll require some help, but I think we can get in, and then do whatever it is that you want to do, Blackhand."

"Good, then let's hear it," Blackhand replied.

"Hold up," La Elfa interrupted, putting her hand up. "If Jack and Pete are setting you up to be killed, and your entire goal is to take out the dukes, then why are we here at Zaragoza? We can just move to Ria Plata and kill the dukes and then come back and remove these two."

"If Jack and Pete were going to be with us, you'd be right. We'd meet with them and then move south right away. But now that we know they are against us, and I had to come here to verify that, we have to cut them out of the picture completely and before we hit the dukes since they know too much. I can't have a second army behind us as we go south to Ria Plata."

La Elfa nodded. "Fair enough. Then let's hear it, Verix," she said, turning to the mage.

"I need to confer with a few people first, then I can give you the plan in the entirety," Verix replied, reaching for an obsidian mirror. "Some old friends from the area," he grinned.

"Fine, but make it quick," Blackhand nodded. "And while you're at it, ask them to see if they can keep an eye out for my would-be assassin."

Verix nodded before walking off to contact his friends.

\* \* \* \* \*

"I need it to be quick and undetectable," Gallo said to a short woman that was walking next to him. "It also can't be traced to me or you."

"Are they ever traced back to us?" the woman joked.

"I just don't want to leave anything to chance. Not on this order," El Gallo replied in a tone that left little question to his meaning.

The woman nodded knowingly at her employer. She was shorter by at least a foot, and slender. She had dark hair and brown eyes. The woman was not very remarkable physically. For the most part, she could blend in with most communities in the world. However, her mind was nearly beyond compare. She had spent decades researching plants and different forms of herbology, becoming a noted healer, but that's not why the Company called upon her.

No one knew where she came from, but River Port had become her home, yet her accent lingered with traces that were more southern than what most in the Tresha region spoke.

"It'll be a lethal dose and fast acting. But the quantity of it, to have it ready so quickly, and then the distribution? Those are questions that I'm not sure you have the time for," she replied.

"There isn't a question of the quantity or the time. I'll leave the method of distribution to you. That's your area of expertise, Doc."

The woman stopped. El Gallo did as well alongside her.

"I'll get this done, but there's something that I'll want besides the normal fee."

"What's that?"

Doc smiled. "I want a favor to be redeemed at a later date."

"A favor?" El Gallo's eyes narrowed.

"A favor from a Company man goes a long way in the world," Doc said, gingerly touching the man's arm.

# 8.

"We can move in tonight," Verix said to Blackhand and the others on the galley.

"The nearest city gate is three miles north of here, so we better start walking then," Blackhand said, standing up. "You can fill us in on the plan along the way."

"I hate walking in without knowing what I should expect," Sergio added.

"I do too," La Elfa agreed. "So, let's hear it Verix."

Verix nodded. "I've contacted some childhood friends. They're the Dockside Gang. I ran with them prior to signing on with Geddoe and his dragon hunters. They pay tribute to the Lord of the City, who we will need to pay off, by the way," Verix stated. "Their leader, Slim Street, is my cousin, and he's agreed to help with the promise that we'll compensate him for any time and damages. He is like the lord of Sala and Zaragoza. At least the underworld part of it."

"Sure, if they swear allegiance to me, and be part of my crew," Blackhand said.

"I figured as much," Verix sighed. "Slim is willing to negotiate, but he's never been one to take orders. However, he's willing to talk because the Lord of the City is trying to stamp his gang out. Being a member of the Company would put an end to that."

"Good," Blackhand replied. "So, they're going to help us, but how will we get in undetected?"

"That's where I'll be doing the most. Once we get close enough, I can cast a fog spell to shroud our approach and entrance."

"Fine then. Let's be off, we're burning daylight out here," Blackhand ordered, leading his huscarls and allies north toward Zaragoza.

The group made their way toward the southern gates of the city. There a man dressed in a brown cloak with his hood up waved them over.

"Verix!" the man said. "It's been too long."

Verix and the man hugged. "It has Dominic," he looked back at Blackhand. "This is Blackhand and part of the crew I told you about. We need to get into the city and past the docks tonight."

"Where you headed from there? Down to that tavern where those Company assholes have posted up at? *The Flying Witch*," Dominic asked.

"That's our business," Blackhand responded. "It's probably safer if you didn't know."

Dominic nodded and eyed Blackhand before answering. "Well, Slim, he's going to want to know. We would rather work with Verix than those other guys. They haven't left that damn bar for two days except to walk the docks once when they first arrived. Besides, if we're doing this for Verix, I think it's fair to say you can trust us."

Blackhand shook his head. "I need more assurance than that."

"Then you'll need to speak to Slim. I can get you in, but from there Slim will have to give you his okay."

Blackhand was about to reply, but Verix stopped him.

"If we can get in now, then we can adapt as needed," Verix said. "Slim just wants to make sure he gets his cut of things, just like you would."

Blackhand sighed. "Fine. Let's get in, and then we can chat with Slim."

Dominic nodded. "Fine by me," he tossed a cord of rope to Blackhand. "You'll need this," he then hoisted a sack from his side and threw it over his right shoulder. "Ready, Verix?"

"For a bit of mischief? Definitely," Verix grinned. He turned to Blackhand. "Once the spell gets going, you'll know it when you see it. Get running to the docks. It's directly to the left once you get in through the gate. They won't see, but be quick, and stay together."

The pair then walked to the side of the gatehouse, passing by two guards that just nodded to Dominic.

"I'm guessing that Slim has these guards paid off," Sergio said.

Blackhand nodded. "That'll be the smart bet."

A few moments later, a deafening boom echoed around the gatehouse, and the sky darkened. A dense fog fell over the city, blinding any passer-by and all those around the area. The fog was heavy, limiting visibility to little more than an arm's length. Its haze was perfect to hide in plain sight, or lack thereof. Blackhand knew the spell for obscuring, but he hadn't seen it used to such effectiveness before. He led his people, each with a portion of the rope in hand as a guideline, through the fog packed city. Blackhand walked in the direction that he had been given and soon found the boat slip off the docks.

"Careful now," Blackhand said. "We need to get the keg or kegs that Pete left for us."

Several of his huscarls walked the area, led by Oreja, who had seen the area where Pete left the kegs. Within a few moments, Oreja walked up to Blackhand, a defused black powder keg in hand.

"We have one, but I could swear he placed two," she said, gently putting the keg down on the ground.

"I don't doubt it. Have your crew find it, but you and I are taking that one to that tavern you said they were at," Blackhand smiled.

Oreja joined Blackhand, Sergio, and La Elfa walking to a high-end brothel away from the docks.

"This is the place they went in. *The Flying Witch*," Oreja said, as the group stood outside a wooden building.

"This is going to be bad," Sergio said.

"It needs to be," La Elfa replied. "Let's just hope Slim is easily compensated."

"Oreja, place the keg where it'll do the worst and run a fuse. Wait for my signal, please," Blackhand said.

Oreja nodded and rushed off to the side of the building to place the keg and run a fuse to a safe distance. Blackhand tried to watch her work, but the fog was still too thick. He wondered if she could tell how far was safe, and if the keg was close enough to their targets, how many other people would be hurt or killed. Too many thoughts rushed through his head.

"I hope Verix is okay," Sergio said, snapping Blackhand from his thoughts.

Blackhand turned to him. "He's home, so I'm imagining he is safe, but we'll meet with him once this is over."

"We'll we be able to find him?" La Elfa asked.

"I'm guessing," Blackhand grinned. "He'll come find us."

Around them, some of Blackhand's men joined them, handing Sergio an armed crossbow. One man had a keg of black powder. Blackhand nodded and grinned once he saw it.

* * * * *

"This is some damned fog that just came up," Pete the Butcher said, peering out of the window on the first floor of *The Flying Witch*.

"Sea fogs float up all the time up north," Jack said from his chair at his table, ignoring the concern in Pete's voice.

"This ain't the north," Pete replied, turning from the window. "This feels unnatural."

Jack put his glass of rum down. "Come on now, this ain't no time to get all superstitious. We're about to be the head men soon."

Pete still looked unconvinced, as the front door burst open, startling everyone in the large room. Even the normally stoic Pete was stunned by the sudden disturbance.

Blackhand, followed by Sergio and La Elfa, walked in. Behind them, a few of Blackhand's huscarls stood armed with daggers and crossbows and all were ready to fight.

"Jack! What a surprise?" Blackhand smirked. He threw his hands in the air as if welcoming a long-lost friend. "And you must be Pete," he said, smiling at the larger man.

"Blackhand, you're a day early," Jack said, his smile fading.

"Yeah, I am. I've also been in touch with El Gallo. He's down south working on a few things for the plan. We brought La Elfa in, too."

Jack nodded softly. "I see that. Welcome," he said sheepishly to the elf woman. "So, Pete and I are… we're ready.

Meet us at the docks and we'll be there shortly."

Blackhand grinned and nodded. "Oh yeah, yeah. That sounds like a brilliant plan. But I need to give you an update, a slight change. I'm taking your business in Larsale. And La Elfa here will be taking your business, Pete."

"Why the hell would I give you or her shit?" Pete asked. "I don't owe you nothing!"

Pete was a giant of a man, red-haired and muscular. He heaved as he breathed, angry and ready to strike. His temper was getting the better of him.

"Well, that's the price for betraying me," Blackhand said.

"That's funny, because this whole thing, us being here, is because you are betraying the Company," Jack replied as he twisted his ruby ring on his index finger

"As are you," Blackhand shot back. "You're working with someone, not sure who, but someone else, and you are leading me into a trap to take my rackets."

"Hell of a story," Jack smiled. "You're reaching."

"Am I?" Blackhand asked. "There are some puzzle pieces missing. I'll give you that, but it makes sense."

"Does it?" Jack smirked. "I think you're scared."

"I think you wanted me dead. You wanted to go through with my plan, but as I talked about it all that day in your office, those wheels in your mind were spinning in another direction. Trying to figure out how you and only you could come out on top.

Pete was your go-to, but he's loyal to Leva. The same duke that set up El Gallo's father. You knew I was going to visit with El Gallo, and with that you have a way to take out half of Millan's family. You don't even need Leva or any other duke's sign off on the killings. We're non-blooded, so who cares, right? You would, in your mind, be seen as loyal to Leva and the other Dukes, but then maybe Leva wants to take out Lord Conrad to rid the Company of the Vasha debts he created. That's what Millan and a few others want to do. All the better, because that means even more money for you and Pete. You just need me dead first," Blackhand explained.

Jack's smirk faded, and he was left looking more concerned than he was when he first saw Blackhand. "Delightful story," Jack said. "But it's just a story."

"And the two kegs at the docks, those are what, just welcoming presents?" Blackhand chuckled. He motioned to the huscarl bringing one keg in. The patrons in the bar, including some soldiers from the Company, all gasped in shock. He looked at Pete. "Look familiar, Pete? It's yours, right?"

"That ain't mine," Pete laughed.

"Who's is it then?" Blackhand smirked.

"Your mothers!" Pete said with a sneer.

"Funny. I figured you planned for me and my crew to get blown up on the docks," Blackhand chuckled.

"I didn't plan nothing."

"Sure, you didn't," La Elfa chuckled. "Jack did, and you're just his stooge."

Blackhand took the keg from his man and walked over to Pete. He put the keg on the table beside Pete and walked back to his men.

"This is what's going to happen," Blackhand began. "You two will stay here until we leave the city. And then you'll disappear. If you don't disappear, then I will kill you. Either way, we take over your crews."

"That's rich," Jack laughed. "You aren't the type to get your hands dirty, Gerald. You're not a killer like us," he said, motioning to Pete and himself. "That's why you needed us. You rather send someone than to do it yourself."

Blackhand pursed his lips, nodding thoughtfully. "Well, true authority never reveals itself," Blackhand replied. "But yeah, you'd think that I don't know how to kill. I let people think that and I'm fine with it. But, yes Jack, I'll kill if I need to. I just don't plan on it today. So, disappear."

Blackhand's tone left nothing to be misunderstood.

"There's no way I'm…" Jack began.

"You won't find a better deal, Jack," Blackhand interrupted. "Don't leave here right now, and I will kill you both."

"Fuck you!" Pete roared, and he rushed toward Blackhand.

La Elfa was quicker and shot a magical burst of energy at Pete, knocking him back onto the wooden floor and against the bar. Pete slumped down, knocked unconscious by the impact. Jack used the distraction to jump up and try to rush out. He turned toward the back door, but Sergio fired a well-aimed crossbow bolt into Jack's leg, stopping the man. Jack fell to the ground and clutched his dagger. He tried to throw it, but one of Blackhand's soldiers kicked it away. Around them, Blackhand's huscarls had fought and subdued Jack and Pete's crews. Several were blooded in the scuffle, and two were unconscious, maybe worse, but either way, they were not in fighting shape.

Sergio walked up to Jack, loading another bolt into his crossbow. He took aim and then fired it into Jack's other leg, leaving him unable to walk.

"Again, disappear Jack. Tell Pete to do the same when he wakes up," Blackhand said as he left the tavern, with his men following behind.

The fog was lifting and more of the city and docks were visible. The group turned a corner, and Blackhand spotted

Oreja. He nodded to her, and she lit the fuse. The spark rushed down the line and in less than twenty seconds later, *The Flying Witch* blew up in a spectacle of timber and splinters.

As the group watched the newly created inferno, Verix ran up to them, Dominic beside him.

"Slim is definitely going to want to talk to you now," Dominic said, his eyes fixated on the tavern, now engulfed in flames.

Around them, people were screaming for help or rushing with water buckets to put out the massive fire.

Blackhand never turned from the scene. "Yeah, we can talk now."

## 9.

Slim wasn't slim. He was a large, robust man in his early forties. His onetime dark hair was beginning to take on the salt and pepper look and his face, with only a couple of slight wrinkles, was chiseled down to the jawline. He held a wooden pipe in his mouth, a plume of aromatic tobacco smoke billowing out.

He stood alongside Blackhand and La Elfa, overlooking the docks. Not too far off, the remains of *The Flying Witch* patrons were being carted off.

"I've run these docks for over a decade. The idea that Pete the Butcher could place a bomb under my nose doesn't sit well with me," Slim said as he looked out on the ships. "That could have wrecked a sizeable portion of my operations here."

Blackhand grinned. "Then I think we did you a favor."

Slim nodded, but he did not smile. "I need to find the leak."

"We can help with that," La Elfa said. "We can be good friends, and we can help each other."

"You want me to get involved in your war?" Slim asked. He noticed the look on the pair's faces and sighed. "You think you and these other Company folks can walk into my city," he motioned to the carts with dead bodies, "and I won't find out why. I have eyes and ears everywhere. Though, I tend to make myself and my crew less visible. Much less visible."

"This was more of a survival tactic," Blackhand replied. "The Company works in the open with very public operations, legitimate, and secretive with the less than legal ones. That's how we have gained our influence over the years."

Slim turned back to the ships sitting on the dock and shook his head. "I heard rumors you weren't the type of man that kills his enemies," Slim said without looking at Blackhand.

"That's true. I honestly would prefer to negotiate. If I can win a battle or war with little to no loss of life, then I feel better," Blackhand replied.

"That's noble," Slim chuckled. "Our lives usually don't allow us such luxuries. Especially here in Zaragoza. That's why we can't always be so open."

"We can help bring you such a luxury," La Elfa said. "It just requires your commitment and trust."

"What? I pay tribute to you and The Company? I run Zaragoza," Slim sternly said. He didn't yell or sound harsh. He didn't need to, but his tone let it be known that he was confident in his words.

"We agree on that," Blackhand clarified. "No, what we want is a partnership. You run Zaragoza. We provide support should you need it, and you do the same if we ask. We all kick up a little bit to the top, which at this point we are still figuring out who that is."

Slim didn't seem convinced. "I'd like to know how to be on the top. What's the process and how safe is it?"

"I think the best option is to have a few of us. No king of kings or duke of dukes. No *Patrón*," Blackhand added. "A council."

Slim nodded. "Okay, like a ruling council, and Zaragoza stays mine?"

"Of course," La Elfa added. "The idea is for all of us, the entire Company to be on the same page and to understand that when we are united three things happen; we make money, we gain influence, and we survive."

"Those are three things that I like," Slim grinned.

"Us too," Blackhand said, extending his hand to Slim. "Are you in?"

Slim nodded and shook Blackhand's hand and then turned and shook La Elfa's. The trio broke off, Blackhand and La Elfa walking back to Sergio and Verix. Sergio handed Jack's ring to Blackhand.

"We pulled it off of one of the bodies. Well, a portion of the body," Sergio said.

Blackhand looked at the ring. Its golden band, though showing some signs of melt from the heat of the powder keg explosion, was still very much intact. The ruby was unaffected.

"Jack did have excellent taste," Blackhand said, marveling at the quality of the ruby ring. "Barely any damage," he looked back to Verix and Sergio. "Any signs of Pete?"

"No real way of identifying any of the bodies. Most were torn apart from the explosion, but I think that, given the length of one leg we found, it probably was him," Sergio replied. "He was a tall guy, and this piece of the leg was longer than others."

"Keep it quiet for now," Blackhand said, he put Jack's ring on his middle finger. "We need a few more days of secrecy until we can strike."

"Speaking of which," La Elfa said, stepping up to Blackhand, "You still owe me a favor."

Blackhand smirked. "Consider it done."

\* \* \* \* \*

The order had come rather clandestinely, and that meant it was of the highest priority. Güero didn't hesitate. He closed up the bar, emptied the safe, the storage trunks of files were removed, and everyone in the entire operation was given new roles in other foreign lands. There were other operations where the workers could make gold and silver, set up new shops, and run their rackets. The gold will still flow.

Güero's specialties were bootleg liquors, gambling, and loan sharking. Those three enterprises could be set up in any port city, or inland city for that matter. However, first he had another job to do.

    Güero came from a long line of Company soldados, and while most of his family were used in more violent capacities, Güero didn't get his hands dirty. He had started, like most others, from the bottom as a page and squire, carrying weapons and gleaming battlefields. Soon enough, however, his skills were noticed, and he was put to use in the battles. Sometime later, Blackhand pulled him out of the rank and file of soldiers once he saw how smart he was. His loyalty was even more needed and sought after. All that said, Güero knew how to do the dirty work if he ever needed to, and now he needed to.

Güero boarded a ship, after wrapping up any loose ends in his bar, and sailed to the port city of Ciudad Topo. Three weeks later, he was walking through the streets of the city, brazen act for a captain from another city. La Elfa's crew knew why he was there and welcomed him. He walked with a pair of them as they followed, from an unseen distance, one of the latest shipments. It was one of the wagon trains that Raton had targeted.

There they saw the wagons get hijacked, as Güero had expected. In front of the wagons, something would obstruct them. One time it was heaps of crates, maybe it was an overturned wagon, and one night several men stood there with crossbows. All tricks to stop the wagons and then clean them out, leaving them empty and the drivers either hurt or dead. At the end, Raton would appear once the danger was over. Güero wanted to see how the thief operated. It was important to watch his moves and mannerisms. Güero did that for several nights, until on the final night, he nodded and had his plan.

"His crews do the work while Raton watches close by. He gives up his protection, thinking that with his crew around him he is protected," Güero said to Jester, La Elfa's loyal second in command. "That's when we'll get him on the next shipment. Two nights, give the word to the rest of the crew."

Jester nodded and followed the order. Two nights later, rounding the corner of a back alley, three wagons moved through the narrow street. Around the wagons men crept from shadows, and in front of the lead wagon a mound of street trash, crates and barrels fell to the ground, blocking the road. The men slowly moved close, but as they stepped into the dim light of the streetlamps, La Elfa's *soldados* appeared from the wagons, crossbows in hand and aimed at the thieves. Behind the third and last wagon, Raton stood, not realizing the danger.

"Oy! What's the holdup?" he yelled out. "Why ain't yall pulling shit off them wagons?!"

Behind him, Raton heard a metallic tapping sound on the cobblestone road. Raton turned to see Güero, cane in hand, walking up to him. He was flanked by two of La Elfa's *soldados*.

"Good evening, Raton," Güero said calmly.

Güero then pulled the handle out of his cane, revealing a thin stiletto blade, and thrust it in and then up into Raton's upper abdomen, through the rib cage, piercing the lung. He retracted the blade and pierced him again, and then a third time for good measure. He let Raton drop to the ground dead, just as Raton's men walked back toward him, pushed along by La Elfa's crossbowmen.

"That's from La Elfa," Güero said, wiping the blade across Raton's shirt to clean off the blood. He looked at Raton's men. "Tonight, your leader paid the price for interfering with Company business. If you don't want to follow him into the afterlife, which I would understand if you don't, then I'd suggest you leave this city immediately. After tonight, if any of you are seen around here, your life is forfeit," Güero motioned for some of La Elfa's *soldados*. "Take some crossbowmen with you and then string Raton's body up in his 'sewer kingdom' as a warning for the rest of his crew. Everyone else, you know the rules about talking too much."

Güero, flanked by two soldados, left the others to do their work and walked back to the docks. He had to board a ship to his next destination.

* * * * *

"Güero just contacted me. It's done," Blackhand said, putting his obsidian mirror away in a satchel.

"Thank you, Gerald. My captain Jester also sent the word up. Things are moving regularly again," La Elfa smiled, sitting at a small table in the stern castle of Blackhand's galley. "I guess I really owe you everything now."

Blackhand shook his head. "Just what we agreed on. We topple the dukes, and then form the council."

"I have news on that, too."

Blackhand looked at La Elfa. She didn't look happy.

"What sort of news?" He asked.

"Fatima was right. The south was purged and the replacements, all blooded, ain't joining. We don't even have to ask them. Their *soldados* might be another story, but we won't know until we act," La Elfa said. "As for the northern *jefes*, with Pete and Jack gone, and you and I taking their crews, we have a better chance. There are eight northern *jefes* left."

"For now, we have to leave Pete and Jack's crews out. Too risky to bring them in and lose our element of surprise," Blackhand added.

"Agreed," La Elfa stood up and poured a goblet of red wine before sitting back down. "With you, me, and Gallo, we need those other eight to either provide soldiers or just wait for us."

"Sergio can reach out to them. He has contacts with most of their crews. I'll set up a meeting with Gallo, but he and I have already worked up a plan," Blackhand said.

"What sort of plan?"

Blackhand shook his head. "I can't say yet. However, in three days, Millan will be here, expecting to meet with me or whoever is meant to kill me before going to Ria Plata. There he wanted to assassinate Conrad. He won't make it to Ria Plata. We will be here to make sure of that."

"Okay, and what about the other dukes?"

"Some in Ria Plata will be taken care of, while others will be met with before arriving," Blackhand said.

La Elfa nodded. "Any that I need to speak with?"

Blackhand shook his head. "No. You, Slim and I will be here when Millan arrives. However, I'd rather you handle it."

La Elfa nodded and then sipped her wine. "Consider it done."

## 10.

El Gallo stepped off his ship in Ria Plata and looked around. He breathed in the salty sea air and grinned. "This will be a very lucrative place to call home soon."

Doc walked up next to him. She grinned as well. "I think I'll like it here."

El Gallo smirked at the woman. "Get set. The dukes will be arriving in the next few days, and your potion has to be ready for them."

"No fear, love," Doc replied. "I and my potion will be ready. As for the others not getting it, do you have that in hand?"

"That's not your concern, Doc. I and my contacts have our orders ready."

The pair, along with several soldados working for El Gallo walked to the inn where they would spend the next week. El Gallo knew that they had one chance at this coup, but he was in the dark with how the other operators were faring. El Gallo shook the thought and worries from his head. He had to focus on his part and let the chips fall as they would.

\* \* \* \* \*

"I've reached out to the other northern *jefes* and their representatives," Sergio said as he, Blackhand, La Elfa, Slim, and Verix sat around Slim's dining room table in his palatial estate.

The stately home was in the hills that ran along the west side of the city-state. Around them, Slim spared no expense showing his taste for the finer things and lasciviousness. Also, all around them, were many guards. When Slim said that he ran Zaragoza, he proved it with the amount of manpower at his disposal. From knights, mages, and men-at-arms, all of them ready to fight for their leader at a moment's notice. Each person at the table had a glass of Zaragozan spiced rum in front of them.

"Four *jefes*, Pecador, Big, Rico, and Red Eye, all swear support. They're sending captains and crews to help with the coming storm. It should be noted that each of these four are non-blooded and had a blooded captain or right hand that turned on them recently. They've been lying low, feeling the same thing we felt," Sergio sipped his rum. He winced at the harshness of the liquid. "Three others, Vera, Logan, and York, also swear allegiance, but are not sending *soldados* because they've got to rebuild after having been hit hard by Vasha or some other force. However, they also have felt the tightening of the dukes and the change in attitudes toward non-bloods."

"Logan is a good man," La Elfa said.

"He's a strong mage, too. This persecution doesn't make sense," Verix added. "Why cut out your best men and women?"

"He's not blooded, and he's an elf. Old animosities are harder to kill than mortals are," Blackhand clarified. "But killing mortals is more expensive. You've said seven, but there are eight others now," Blackhand said, looking at Sergio. "What of Buccan?"

Sergio lowered his head and shook it. "Buccan's gone. His right hand took him out and has taken over operations."

"That's not good," La Elfa said. "Any chance he found out what we are doing?"

"It's possible, but I don't think it'll matter," Sergio replied. "I didn't mention anything, if that's what you're wondering."

"Of course not. I didn't think you did," La Elfa clarified.

"Let's move on," Blackhand said, sensing the building tension.

"I have a question," Slim spoke up, also wanting to ease the tension.

"Please," Blackhand said.

"How does the Company work, given all of the less than legitimate operations and still being the most powerful mercenary company as a public force?" Slim asked. "And now I'm going to be involved. How do we get recruits?"

"That's a good question," Blackhand smiled. "The military operations are the start of it all, really. That's where Sergio and I got our start. We were two-bit thieves in the Free Cities, saw that The Company was hiring on pages. We signed up, because it meant guaranteed meals and warm places to sleep. Sergio and I spent the next couple of years carrying water, weapons, or bodies on battlefields until we were put into the fights. That's how you become a Company man-at-arms. Then you start making gold so that you can buy quality arms and armor."

"And the other operations?"

Blackhand nodded. "That comes when a man-at-arms gets noticed. The military side has the ranks just like others, sergeant, lieutenant, and so on, but a Company Captain is different. They notice you and call for your help. It's often a test.

Do a good job, keep your mouth shut, and then they'll test you again. And again, until they think you're worth bringing into their fold. At that point, you'll work for the captain and only that captain. You'll be expected to follow the orders and find new avenues and streams of income. Do well enough and you become a captain yourself, and then perhaps a *jefe*. Sergio and I have been through it all, so when I was named *jefe*, I placed him as my castellan, which is basically my right hand."

"So, I'll recruit soldiers for the army, and then observe them for other things?" Slim asked. "As I always have observed people for such uses?"

"Exactly," Sergio answered.

Blackhand nodded and smiled. "Back to it then. Tomorrow Millan will be here, expecting me to be dead," he looked at

Slim. "To that end, have your men found my assassin?"

Slim grinned. "We did indeed."

The group left Slim's dining room and followed him through the massive estate. They rounded corners and walked down halls until they reached a large wooden door. It was fitted with wrought iron and magically sealed. Slim placed his palm in the center and the door locks clicked open. He opened the door and led everyone through the doorway and down a wooden staircase and into the mansion's cellar.

"We caught him stalking you the first day you got into the city," Slim said as he lit a candle. He touched the candle to a wall torch. That torch blazed with a fire that lit other torches around the room. "He started talking about four hours into us roughing him up," Slim walked to a hooded man tied up and hunched over in a chair in the center of the cellar.

Slim pulled the hood off to reveal the man's bruised and bloody face.

"I know him," Blackhand said. "He was part of my crew. Captain Cortes."

The man in the chair was, until that moment, one of Blackhand's best captains and most loyal. Only behind Sergio and Güero. Captain Cortes controlled the operations within the Lotcalan coast and eastern Panyakuta. Mostly running weapons and brothels. He also commanded over two thousand mercenary troops, known as the Black Corps.

"This is very disappointing," Blackhand continued. "I trusted you, Enrique," he said, using Cortes' first name. "Let me guess, it isn't personal, just business?"

Cortes lifted his head up to look at Blackhand. He spit at his former boss.

"*Eres una sangre falsa,*" he whispered. "We are cleansing the Company of the fakes like you."

"I guess it is personal, then. So, you had to come and do the job yourself? A captain doing a regular hit isn't normal. Very irregular," Blackhand said.

"You're not a regular man, Gerald. You're the fabled *Blackhand*," Cortes mocked. "The man that has never lost a battle. The man that is always lucky and always making the right moves. Everyone on the streets says that you walk through the underworld and give the king of the dead orders. Yes, I came to do the job to make sure it was done right."

"Two things," Blackhand began. He pulled at Cortes' hair, pulling his head back and revealing his eyes. "You didn't do the job right if you got caught before you completed the mission, therefore you're just a two-bit asshole traitor. Second, if I am the sort of man that's never lost a battle and the one that's always making the right moves, why did you betray me?"

Cortes chuckled. "You're not one of us. You should be taking my orders. Besides, your luck will run out one day."

"Not today," Blackhand said.

"Boss," Sergio stepped next to Blackhand. "We have to kill him. There's only one answer to disloyalty."

"Yeah."

"I'll do it," La Elfa said.

"No," Sergio responded. "I will," his voice dripping with anger and hatred. "I can't stand traitors, and this is worse than just some punk running his mouth. We've broken bread more times than I can count. *¡Éramos Hermanos!*" Sergio sneered at Cortes.

Blackhand shook his head. "No. I will. He came for me. I was the target," Blackhand said. "I'll do it."

Cortes tried to squirm free, but the rope used to tie him to the chair was too tight and thick to break free. Blackhand pulled a dagger out and ran the edge of the blade across Cortes' throat. The man gurgled blood, gasping for air, but that rapidly ended as his life drained from him. Cortes' head slumped down to his chest, dead and gone.

"How do you normally get rid of bodies here in Zaragoza?" Blackhand asked Slim.

"Pigs. We feed them to the pigs. They'll eat pretty much anything," Slim answered with a wicked grin. He waved for two of his men to retrieve the body and dispose of it. "We'll take care of it."

Blackhand nodded and then turned to face Sergio and La Elfa. "From now on, any death like this has to be a council decision. He was high ranking and once a valuable member of our family. This is the last killing based on emotion."

"Who's the council?" La Elfa asked.

"Right now, us here in this room, and the other *jefes* that join us. Verix, if you want in, we can discuss it," Blackhand said.

Verix shook his head. "I'm just here for the time being. I'll keep your secrets and oaths, but I rather not run any crews."

"Fair enough. Just remember what you just promised about our secrets," Blackhand replied.

Sergio looked at Verix. "Because we won't forget."

Verix nodded his understanding of the warning, especially after what he had just witnessed.

## 11.

Slim walked along the dockyard with Blackhand. The pair were bathed in the warm glow of the morning sun, though the air around them was crisp and cool because of the coming winter season. It was in moments like this that one had to enjoy the sun while it was around before the snow clouds obscured it. Both were enjoying the quiet and calm respite from the action that was going on around them. Workers loaded freight and barrels onto wagons and or ships, fishermen were unloading their catches from the previous night, and the fishmongers were yelling out their goods.

Slim and Blackhand wanted to iron out all the finer details. For Slim, who had been on his own for years, had to now get used to being part of something bigger and with more rules than his usual operation.

"I kick up a percentage of my wages to you, and I get what again for those efforts?" Slim asked, trying to finalize any business talks and seeing if the deal was really worth it for him.

Blackhand smiled. "A seat at the table with the other *jefes* and a portion of the Company's considerable assets and manpower should you need it. We'll station a corps of soldiers here that you'll command, in case anyone in the region wants to hire them for battles or protection."

"I'll be called upon in various disputes among kings, counts, nobles and what not?"

"Is that a problem?" Blackhand asked.

Slim shook his head. "Zaragozan mercenaries are well sought after. Pay would be proportionate?"

"Payment would be within current Company standards," Blackhand answered. "Those Zaragozan mercenaries, mainly the independent ones, would be a good place to recruit from. We might also ask for Zaragozan holdings to expand our physical reach as well. Castles, fortifications, perhaps small hamlets. In the best interest of the Company, of course."

"And I'll get a taste of that?" Slim asked.

"Of course," Blackhand smiled. "Anything coming in or out of the city will be subject to a fee that you'll manage and then kick up a small percent."

"How small?"

"We'll hammer those details out later," Blackhand said. "Above all, since you spoke the oath, I'll reiterate that it's Company first, and above all else. No other personal matters will be placed before the Company. The Company is your family now, we are your life for the remainder of it, and the only priority is whatever the Company priority is. We won't tolerate lies between us. From now on, we have to honor one another because, as the Company, we are one force stronger than any king, emperor, or nation."

Slim nodded and grinned. "That I like, and I suppose that's worth the sacrifice of some of my independence."

Blackhand smiled and patted his new partner on the shoulder. "We're all in the same boat. All equal on this level," Blackhand pointed to the docks, drawing

Slim's attention back to their focus. "For now, we have to prepare the city for Duke Millan's arrival."

Slim nodded. "What do you need from me?"

"Soldiers, and a place to dispose of whoever he brings along."

"Done," Slim smiled. "I like you, Gerald. You are a veteran of war. You know what some of us have been through. But you're also pragmatic and understanding. So I hate to ask this, but I need a favor, if you can spare the time."

"Sure," Blackhand said.

"It's a loan that I gave to my brother-in-law, Chucho. He hasn't paid it back in over a year. I gave him a long leash, but he is insulting my kindness."

"I understand," Blackhand said. "Where can I find him?"

"You're going to do it yourself?"

"I'll also be sending Sergio. He is better at collecting than I am. But I'll be with him."

"He runs a textile mill and warehouse in the northern part of the city. You'll find him there and maybe he disappears. I can't have him walking around here any longer, at least. It's bad for my image. He owes me five hundred silver, so I want that back, and you can keep ten percent," Slim said. "They call him, Big Ears."

"Done," Blackhand replied.

What happened next was a whirlwind of action. Blackhand burst into the textile warehouse, and Sergio led the huscarls through the secret entrance with the force of ten larger men!

"Where is Big Ears!" Sergio yelled out. Blackhand was behind him with a crossbow aimed.

Around them, a bunch of women, mostly darker skinned women of Zaragozan ancestry, screamed out in shock and pointed to a back room.

"In there, boss," Segio said to Blackhand.

Blackhand and Segio both walked through the office and found the young man.

"You Big Ears?" Blackhand asked. His crossbow was raised and pointed at the man.

The man nodded, scared and ready to run.

"I know your brother-in-law is a hothead, but you owe him a chunk of change!" Blackhand said. "You know that we have to end this insult now."

"I can pay. Five hundred silver, right? I have that," Big Ears said.

"I'm sure you do, and we'll take that too, but you have to serve as an example," Blackhand said. He fired the crossbow bolt into Big Ears' eye, killing the man.

Blackhand turned to Sergio. "Find the safe or lockbox. We'll take the coin," Blackhand whistled for the huscarls outside the office. "Two of you, take Big Ears here, weigh him down, and dump his body in the bay. The rest of you, take these women and have them put to work for Slim."

Sergio walked up to Blackhand, dragging a large sack of jingling coins. "Did a quick count and stopped at five hundred.

There's more," he said, finding a cart to load the heavy sack onto.

"Then Slim gets his five and we get the rest," Blackhand grinned.

\* \* \* \* \*

The day came. Millan was stepping off of his ship, expecting to be greeted by Captain Enrique Cortes. Duke Millan was escorted by Captain Miguel Cobarde, a blooded captain that used to be under El Gallo and now recruited for Millan.

Millan was dressed in his usual finery, with the Company emblem embroidered on his chest. Cobarde was more well equipped for what he thought might be a dangerous situation. He had an iron chest plate, thick leather padded trousers and tunic.

A few men-at-arms flanked the pair. It wasn't an impressive force in size, but each of the members of Millan's group was indeed skilled and deadly. Millan walked the docks, peering around for anything out of place. He hadn't heard from either Blackhand or Cortes, though in his mind he would rather have heard from Cortes. However, no word was passed to him from either.

Millan wasn't as familiar with Zaragoza as he was with other cities. Zaragoza hadn't been in Company control, not for lack of trying. Millan had heard some grumbling that El Gallo had left and disappeared, and a few other *jefes* were becoming scarce. While Millan had started his own purge, his plan was only just beginning to see fruit. Buccan was the first *jefe* to fall to Millan's blooded plan, but the other captains hadn't reported back. That meant that each step had to be exactly in line with his plan.

"Once we're done here, we'll move to Ria Plata. I have to make sure that Cortes was able to strike against Blackhand. Assuming that, he'll take over those loyal captains, and you'll run Gallo's crews," Millan explained to Cobarde.

Cobarde nodded. "Sounds good, sir."

The pair stepped onto the stone street and glanced around. They didn't see their Company counterparts, only dock workers going about their daily lives. Loading wagons, ships, and carts. Moving cargo bound for many different locales throughout the world. Millan noticed the goods, cotton, tobacco, and oils, all lucrative cash goods. His eyes were already scheming for more wealth.

To his left, he missed the figure that strolled up to him.

"You're right on time, boss."

Millan turned, startled when he recognized the voice as his *jefe,* Blackhand.

"I know you were expecting Cortes," Blackhand said, putting his hands up in a shrug. "He is unavailable."

"What did you do?" Millan asked, still in shock at the sight. "Where is Cortes?"

"I'm told that here in Zaragoza they dispose of bodies by throwing them to the pigs."

Millan gulped a breath. Cobarde sneered.

"You dirt blood bastard!" the captain yelled out. "Attack him!" Cobarde ordered.

The men-at-arms rushed close, but several dock workers stepped up and blocked them. A scuffle started, but the dock workers were already armed with daggers, expertly stabbing at unarmored portions of the men-at-arms' bodies. Even though one of the dock workers was wounded with a knife to the gut, none had been killed, while the men that Millan had brought were all laying dead on the street.

"You should have brought more men," Blackhand taunted.

Sergio, La Elfa, Verix, and Slim walked up next to Blackhand. They stood with him, none of them looking happy. Sergio stood with an armed crossbow.

"We're not too thrilled about your purge idea. We thought we had an accord," Blackhand began. "But it's a long time coming, so we are striking first. With the exception of *Jefe* Buccan, we have the support of each of the northern jefes, and Leva's *jefes*. This also now includes *Jefe* Jack Kelly and Pete's crews."

"You have nothing, Gerald," Millan smirked.

"No, we have everything," La Elfa corrected. "And once we're finished, no duke will be left."

"You can't kill all the dukes," Cobarde said. "You're just a *gringo* piece of shit that we blessed with a position. You should be begging for your life right now."

"Kill him," Blackhand ordered.

In an instant, Sergio lifted his crossbow and fired the bolt into Cobarde face, piercing his unprotected forehead. The man dropped to the ground in a heap of iron plate and limp flesh.

"Get the ship cleared out and let's find out the loyalties," Blackhand ordered.

Slim ordered his men to the task, and they began pulling each crew member out, interrogating them for their worth. Blackhand and his fellow crew watched the scene. Millan just stood there, all the while never taking his eyes off of Blackhand. A few of Millan's sailors were put to the sword for their answers, but slowly others understood the point of it all.

"So, what's your play, Gerald?" Millan asked.

"I take over all of your operations and form a new council with the remaining *jefes*. We'll make the Company feared and respected again," Blackhand said.

"There are too many dukes to take out for you to be able to do something like that," Millan replied with a chuckle. "So, you'll betray your own boss, your friend?"

Blackhand nodded. "You always said that when someone joins up, the only way out is death," Blackhand pointed at Millan. "You told me that when that time comes, it'll be from behind with a Company dagger. You tried that with me, but I found your betrayal first."

Millan shook his head. "You aren't strong enough to take on the entire Company."

"We don't intend to do it alone," La Elfa said, pulling out her dagger. "But we've said enough as it is."

She stepped up to Millan and shoved her dagger into Millan's abdomen. She twisted the blade deep into the man and then jerked it free. Millan dropped to his knees in front of La Elfa. She took her dagger and thrusted it into Millan's chest, piercing his heart before pulling the bloody blade back out. Millan fell to the ground, blood oozing from his body.

Slim called over a few of his men. "Bring a wagon and remove the bodies."

Blackhand knelt down next to Millan. He pulled off the livery collar from around the dead duke's neck and took the ring off of Millan's finger. Blackhand put the ring in his pocket and stuffed the collar into his satchel.

Blackhand looked at his companions. "Time to let the others know how to proceed. I'll need an obsidian mirror to call in a favor," he said, looking at Verix.

## 12.

Doc put on her stolen chamberlain outfit. The dukes had started arriving and now the final portion of Blackhand's plan was in the works. Doc had arrived at the opulent castle that housed the dukes. There she was able to sneak in, find a noble-looking outfit and a crest of the chamberlain, and blend in with the other servants. She pulled out several small vials of a translucent blue liquid from a pocket sewn into her dress and rushed into the kitchen.

"Come now, ladies!" Doc ordered. "Them nobles ain't going to enjoy being kept waiting."

The other servants, mostly cooks and maids, all turned to regard the unfamiliar voice.

"What?" Doc said. Her tone was stern, and her face showed no empathy for the hard work of a castle kitchen maid or cook.

"Who are you, ma'am?" one of the cooks asked. He was a large man, stout and older. A greying bushy beard framed his rough face. His hands, callused from wear, looked poised to strike.

Doc lowered her head in a menacing stare at the man. "I am the steward of Duke Millan and have been overseeing his travel arrangements for ten years. I just arrived, and my only goal here," she started walking toward the cook, "is to make sure that these dukes are well fed and happy so they can conduct Company business because if there are any distractions, then heads will usually roll and I assure you that mine will not be one of them," Doc looked the man up and down, and stabbed his chest with her index finger. "Now, you tell me, is there a problem, chef?"

The man shook his head rapidly.

"Good. Get back to work. I want those pies on the table in thirty minutes!" Doc ordered.

"Yes, ma'am," all the servants called out.

Doc smiled and left the cooks and maids to their business. On her way out, she got a good look at the parchment detailing the breakfast and lunch routines for the dukes.

Outside the castle, four *soldados*, who looked blooded but were not, under the orders of *Jefes* Gallo, Pecador, and Red Eye, walked into the castle, showing their credentials as members of the Company.

One of the soldados, Marcus, pulled the others to the side when Doc turned the corner and motioned for them to join her. Once secluded, Doc laid out the plan to eliminate the factions.

"We have to be quick," Doc began. "All the dukes are here except Conrad, Millan, and Leva. El Gallo has Leva, and Blackhand is taking care of Millan, so that leaves Conrad, and the dukes that are here."

"How many dukes are here?" Marcus asked.

"Fifteen. two, however, have refused breakfast. You four will have to take care of them. I'll handle the other thirteen," Doc answered. "You can find them throughout the estate or in the bathhouse. I heard that Duke Roberto likes morning rides, so he might be out on the grounds. I saw Orsino pestering a maid near the bathhouse. Maybe he's still there, distracted."

Marcus and the others nodded in agreement.

"Meet back at the ship then, gentlemen," Doc said before walking off toward the dining room.

Marcus and the others rushed off to find their assigned dukes. Doc made her way into the dining room and helped to prepare the room. Servers brought out trays of pies and fruits. Along the wall were decanters of water and wine.

"A fine toast," Doc smirked. She waited until the room was empty and she pulled out her vials. "This should be more than enough for quick deaths."

Doc poured the contents of the vials into each of the decanters of water and wine.

She was putting the final vial away when the first duke, Gomez, arrived. He offered a curt and unfriendly smile to Doc, who simply curtsied. Behind him, other dukes started to enter the room. A few motioned for Doc to serve them their breakfast. She motioned for other maids to do the honors, while she began pouring goblets of wine once she had counted the twelve dukes, she had been expecting were all in attendance. Each happily took the offered wine goblets. Doc placed the final one down and then strolled out of the room and toward the exit as each of the dukes began offering meaningless toasts to success. She grinned when she heard one starting to clear his throat, and then others did the same. But within a minute Doc was out of the back door, even so she could hear the screaming from the maids.

Away from the dining room, Tommaso and his partner, Carlo, both representatives of *Jefe* Pecador, walked into a bathhouse where Duke Orsino was enjoying a hot bath. They motioned to the woman that was washing him away, startling the duke. She ran out of the door once she saw Tommaso flash his dagger.

"What? Who the hell are you two?" Orsino asked, trying to stand, but Carlo held him down. "What the fuck do you think…"

"Shut up, Orsino," Tommaso said in a rough voice. "This is from our *Jefe*, *Señor* Pecador," he said before stabbing the duke while he was held down in the tub. Tommaso thrust the dagger into the duke's chest again and then pulled the bloody blade out.

Carlo pushed the duke below the water, for good measure. The pair watched as the duke's body went still in the hot water. Tommaso looked at Carlo and nodded. The pair took the duke's ring and collar before walking out of the bathhouse and leaving the estate.

Duke Roberto was away on his horse with his wife, enjoying an early morning ride before breakfast. Marcus and his partner, a man named Genero, walked up to the duke and waited for his attention. Duke Roberto saw the pair, thinking it was strange, but he trotted his horse toward the two men, seeing how they were Company men by their coat of arms.

"Gentlemen, may I help you?" Roberto said with a friendly smile.

Marcus grabbed the horse's reins and pulled out his dagger. "We have a message from *Jefes* Gallo and Red Eye, *cabrón*!"

The duke didn't have time to react as Marcus sunk his dagger into the horse's neck, making the animal rise and back. The horse fell to the ground and landed on top of the duke. Genero rushed over and cut through the stuck duke's neck, nearly cutting the duke's head off. He took the ring and collar from the duke. In the midst of it all, the duke's wife was calling out and screaming for help. She rushed over to try to attack the pair, but Marcus pulled her from her horse and knocked her unconscious, leaving her prone on the ground. Marcus grabbed Genero, and the pair ran for the estate's walls and climbed out just as men with crossbows unleashed their bolts. A bolt hit Genero in the calf, but Marcus pulled him up and over, allowing the pair to escape into a nearby side alley and then sewer.

Doc, Carlo, and Tommaso heard the commotion as they met up near the docks. Doc grinned.

"We knew they'd catch on. Time for Gallo to end it with Leva," she said as the trio walked to Gallo's ship.

## 13.

Duke Leva had arrived later than the other dukes and was just walking off his ship when he stepped closer to the dockyard. The normally busy docks were empty and quiet. The usual market stalls were empty and crates, barrels, and other goods were simply sitting unattended.

Duke Leva shrugged the unusual emptiness off and kept his mind focused on getting to the castle estate. From the docks, he spied a familiar face in front of him.

"You're Duke Millan's *jefe*, the rooster one. Right?" Leva asked, seeing Gallo's face.

Leva was a shorter man, stocky, with dark hair cut short. He was flanked by two men-at-arms while Gallo was alone.

Gallo nodded. "I am. I'm also the son of *Jefe* Hidalgo, who everyone called 'Redmayne'," he patted the stock of the crossbow he held in his hands. "This was his crossbow, and one he used very effectively until you had him murdered."

Leva eyed Gallo. His eyes narrowed at the sound of Gallo's father's name. He nodded, understanding.

"So, you've come to settle a vendetta against me? Millan won't allow it," Leva chuckled.

Gallo shook his head. "Millan is dead. Blackhand saw to that. All the other dukes are dead, too," Gallo said. "You and Conrad are all that's left. Once you two are dead, the remaining *jefes* will run the company."

Leva's laugh faded. He looked stunned. "That's impossible. That would be too difficult for a couple of *jefes* to accomplish."

Gallo smirked. "It's not just a couple of *jefes*," Gallo jerked his head to the side, motioning for the two men with Leva to leave. Both nodded and walked up the dock and past Gallo. "We've made some deals. It seems that other *jefes* and captains didn't like the southern purge you, and the other dukes, tried to pull off."

"So, you want to negotiate a better deal or something?" Leva sneered.

"No," Gallo said, as he lifted his crossbow and fired a bolt into Leva's face. The bolt pierced the duke's brain, and he fell back onto the docks. Gallo walked over to him, knelt down, and removed the duke's ring and collar.

"No deals," he said, before rolling the duke over the edge of the dock and into the cold water. He turned to see Marcus and Genero exiting a sewer pipe and running, rather limping in Genero's case, toward Gallo's ship. A grin ran across his face.

\* \* \* \* \*

Duke Conrad sat in his stateroom, atop the main keep of his castle in Ria Plata. All around him, he had heard the screams from his servants, and news was that all the dukes that were under him were now dead. News had reached him of Leva's death and just a few moments prior, his chamberlain was found dead. Now, the rumor was that Millan was dead as well and that the Vasha oligarchs were no longer waiting for gold and were sailing to Ria Plata looking for payment. Either Conrad's gold or his blood.

Conrad's hand was shaking as he tried to drink from his goblet, but he couldn't. Something within himself was holding him back. He was disheveled and weeping as he attempted and failed again to drink from the goblet. Behind him, a purple portal opened up and closed after a feminine figure walked out.

"Can't do it, can you?" the woman asked.

Conrad turned in a start, his goblet falling to the floor and spilling the liquid. "Wha…"

"What is that? Essence of nightshade, widow's leaf?" the woman asked, picking up the goblet and smelling what was left of the contents. "Excellent methods that are painless. Perfect for a coward like you," she tossed the silver cup to the floor.

"Who are you?" Conrad asked.

"I'm someone that you've hurt. My family was torn apart by your last war, and I'm here to make sure that no one else is hurt by your stupidity again. I had retired, as well as my crew, but one last job brought us back out. One special one. Just so you are aware, my hit squad is cleaning up the remains and purging the castle servants as we speak. No witnesses, per the usual rules."

"Who…"

"They call me Lestrade *de la Flor Venenosa*, and you had my father murdered and ordered the same for my brother," she replied, pulling the collar of the old man's robe, pulling him close to her face. "This is for them, and it's also from my friend Blackhand, who bids you well," Lestrade said, letting Conrad fall back into his chair, before sinking her dagger deep into

Conrad's stomach. She pulled the blade out and sliced his throat.

Lestrade cleaned the blade off on Conrad's tunic and then opened a new portal and walked through it. When she walked out, she was in Zaragoza and standing in front of Blackhand and several other *jefes*.

"The castle is yours," Lestrade said with a stern look. "And I'm now, officially, out."

Blackhand nodded. "Go in peace."

Lestrade returned the nod and then conjured another portal and disappeared within it to parts unknown.

## 14.

Two weeks passed, and though the Company operations continued as normal, things were still being figured out. Gallo arrived in Zaragoza and treated with the other *jefes*. The southern *jefes* that had been installed after the purge were subject to their own betrayal. Each was murdered by their captains under the orders of Blackhand and the members of the council. The replacements, loyal to the council, and the Company, joined Blackhand and the others in Zaragoza in the remaining days and weeks.

Soon, the twenty-one *jefes* were in Slim's luxurious estate in the hills of Zaragoza. It was a meeting held at midnight with the highest-ranking members of the Company. It was also mandatory that each attend. Each *jefe* was adorned in the livery collar of their station, and all had the Company coat of arms on their left breast of their coat, and their personal arms on the right breast. Behind them, their captains stood, all also wearing their finest attire, and all watching intently.

The room was dim, with only one candle lit, as each of the jefes stood around a circular table in the middle of the room. Blackhand stood in front of a paper that he had brought with him.

"As we can all see, the ruling body of the Company is now us, the council," Blackhand began. "No longer an organization bound by blood to a homeland, but through loyalty of service and sacrifice. We are all blooded because we've bled with one another at some point or another. However, I want to make sure we all know the depth of these oaths that we have retaken tonight. On this parchment is the symbol of our organization and each of our names," Blackhand drew his dagger and sliced his left palm, drawing a line of blood. He dripped it onto a parchment with their names, and the Company coat of arms. "I swear that I am a man of the Company from this day until my last and will never turn my back on it or my brethren on the pain of a traitor's death."

The other *jefes* all stood, daggers in hand, and cut their palms, letting the blood drop on the same parchment as it was passed around in front of each of them. In the end, each *jefe's* blood soaked into the parchment, and over the Company coat of arms.

"We're all bound to the same fate now," La Elfa said. "Let it be known this day forward that any man or woman who wishes to rise in the ranks must take this same oath. Your captains will now take this oath," she said, reaching for a new parchment, "and then your officers will be asked to give the same promises."

Once each captain spoke the oath and made the same gestures with their daggers and blood upon the parchment, the room fell into a solemn silence.

La Elfa then cast a fire spell and lit all the candles in the room. Around them, a feast was laid out. "Now, we'll break bread and be as one, again as those that founded our brotherhood once did," she smiled.

\* \* \* \* \*

After a few arduous months of breaking in the new *jefes*, and gathering the intel on any disloyal members, Blackhand settled into a comfortable rhythm back in Aran. The Vasha oligarchs were still very much a problem. However, with a stronger organization showing force, none of the old enemies from the Vasha region seemed to be eager to fight. That gave the Company a bit of a respite, even if it would just be temporary.

Sergio joined Blackhand in Aran, and for the most part, business returned to usual. Though some felt that some bad blood might still linger, nothing came from it since the night each took their oaths, now referred to as the Midnight Oaths. That was another blessing for the newly formed and already busy council.

"Sergio?" Blackhand said, looking out over the estate that he called home. "We need to look south again."

Sergio was behind him, concentrating on papers and letters at his desk, trying to determine a good next move.

"Our fellow Company men are established and reestablished as we speak. Gallo is holding Ria Plata well and has already transitioned the operations from Conrad to his own and distributed some of the lines of income to Güero."

"Yes, all well and good. However, I'm thinking further south."

Sergio put his papers down, as a maid brought in two cups of coffee, and a pitcher.

"How far south?" Sergio asked, accepting the cup from the maid. He motioned for her to leave and close the door.

The maid closed the door behind her before Blackhand began to speak.

"Nashoba," Blackhand said with a smile as he turned to look at Sergio.

Sergio smirked. "Well," he said as he stood up. "It just so happens that I have a letter here from a very motivated mercenary captain requesting soldiers in that very region."

Blackhand's grin grew wider. "Do you now?"

"Rowena has formally asked for Company support," Sergio said, handing the letter to Blackhand. "And willing to pay her weight in gold."

"I think that's a fine offer," Blackhand said, accepting the letter. "I think I see a new source of income for us in the near future and I think I'll visit her personally," he grinned.

THE COMPANY | **194**

## About the Author

Joseph S. Samaniego is a historian from North Carolina specializing in medieval European History. He has a Master of Arts in History and has future plans to receive a PhD.

In his daily life, he is not only a Fantasy author with multiple titles to his credit, but he also writes non-fiction and is a gifted fantasy cartographer.

When he is not spending time with his family, Joseph spends time reading, writing and playing video games.